THE BODYGUARD MAN

Suddenly the music in the night-club came to a halt. For the space of a second the girl stared pointedly in the direction of our table before her hands moved down slowly over her breasts and across her ribs towards her hips – and the room was blanketed in darkness.

I slammed my arms outwards and felt both Corrente and Tozzi jerk off balance. My mind registered a flat whirring noise that cut past my right shoulder, and the world became a jumble of sharp impressions. In the split-second after the spotlight again came on, I looked at the girl. She was standing where she had been before, the G-string now missing – but the knife had entered her body only millimetres above her pubic hair, and had buried itself to the hilt. Her eyes had snapped wide open.

'Told by a young British agent, tough as a modern tot's fantasy. Lapsed from the Special Branch, he is employed by a Florentine manager to protect brilliant Sardinian footballer, an exhibitionist with problems . . .'
Observer

'Much information, much mystification'
H. R. F. Keating in The Times

'Harry Mann fancies himself a bit as an ex-Special Branch desperado, and there are signs that this aspires to more than thriller status . . . it's got punch and bite'
Evening Standard

**Also by the same author,
and available from Coronet**

PLAYING THE WILD CARD

About the author

Philip Evans was born in Colombo, educated in
Ootacamund, Newbury, Bath and Oxford, has
written three novels, NEXT TIME YOU'LL
WAKE UP DEAD (1972), THE BODYGUARD
MAN (1973) and PLAYING THE WILD CARD
(1988), as well as several books about football, and
lives in London with his wife, and two daughters.

The Bodyguard Man

Philip Evans

CORONET BOOKS
Hodder and Stoughton

For Christopher and
Diana

Copyright © 1973, 1990 by Philip
Evans

First published in Great Britain in
1973 by Hodder and Stoughton Ltd.

Coronet edition 1990

Printed and bound in Great Britain
for Hodder and Stoughton
Paperbacks, a division of Hodder and
Stoughton Ltd, Mill Road,
Dunton Green, Sevenoaks, Kent
TN13 2YA (Editorial Office: 47 Bedford
Square, London WC1B 3DP) by R. Clay
Ltd, Bungay, Suffolk

British Library C.I.P.

Evans, Philip, *1943 Apr. 4-*
The bodyguard man.
I. Title
823'.914 [F]

ISBN 0-340-51596-1

FIORENTINA — NOTES FROM A SUPPORTER

Associazione Calcio Fiorentina s.p.a. was founded in 1926. The club has had many fine players at its disposal in recent years, but none remotely resembling the 'Gianni Corrente' of the story, and I have yet to meet a manager or director of the club who can claim similarity to either 'Dino Tozzi' or to 'Giorgio Belmonte'. This is a work of fiction and should be read as such.

In fact the germ of this novel was implanted on 12th October 1969 when I accompanied a former player to the Stadio Communale in Florence to watch a match between the home team and Cagliari. Advance interest in the game was high. Fiorentina had won the 1968/9 *scudetto*, Cagliari had finished in second place, and after four games in the new season both were again at the top of the league. In addition to seeing several players who would be vying for places in the Italian squad for the World Cup Qualifying match against Wales three weeks later, the capacity crowd of 52,000 spectators was very aware that the team from Sardinia fielded no fewer than four players who in the past had represented the Tuscan side – and supporters of any team usually relish the chance of watching former heroes struggle!

Four days earlier another friend had taken me to watch AC Milan's 3-0 home leg victory against Estudiantes of Buenos Aires, victors in the World Club Championship of the previous year against Manchester United. There had been much passion in the contest as well as a nerve-tingling amount of tension. This was primarily due to some savage tackling by certain members of the visiting side, prominent for whom had been Carlos Bilardo, who four years ago steered Argentina to victory in the 1986 World Cup. However the match between Fiorentina and Cagliari was the first I saw between teams that were both Italian, and also on the field was Concetto Lo Bello, a much-praised and straight-backed referee who'd officiated during the 1966 World Cup and for whom all players held great respect. Always seen close to the play, he remained one never carried away by events, and strode around the pitch with the bearing of an aristocrat mingling with his vassals.

Referees have certain locales which they always like to visit, but the Stadio Communale could not conceivably have been a favoured ground of Concetto Lo Bello – and decidedly not after this match. He cast away any lingering popularity he might have had with the home crowd by awarding Cagliari a penalty minutes after the game's start. Although there followed the usual concerto of pleadings and protests, Lo Bello remained inflexible in his decision, and Luigi Riva scored with his fabled left foot.

Never mind, the supporters thought as they settled back in their seats, *non importa*. Fiorentina could still score the equaliser – and then who knows? They soon realised that Concetto Lo Bello did, for one. When a Fiorentina player was taken down in the Cagliari penalty area, the referee waved play on in an imperious manner; and when another slid the ball past Enrico Albertosi in the Cagliari goal, Lo Bello disallowed the score since a colleague was in an offside position, although the Fiorentina fans must have thought that in no manner could he have been 'interfering with the play'. 1-0 to Cagliari, then, was the final score, and it came as no great surprise to find Lo Bello requiring

6

a police escort after the final whistle, nor to learn that he was besieged in his dressing room for more than two hours after the game.

That match, however, struck me as being the most majestic piece of theatre, with much skilful football being served up to the spectators, much of it orchestrated by Giancarlo De Sisti, Fiorentina's playmaker, who was one of seven players in that game who went on to contribute to Italy's effort in the World Cup finals in 1970 when the team was beaten in the actual Final by Brazil. As well as having inspiring football, the contest also contained an immense amount of drama, in addition to an authoritative performance as referee by Concetto Lo Bello.

THE BODYGUARD MAN was written during 1972 and first published in 1973, with paperback rights being purchased by Panther. Expectation further mounted as the film rights were purchased by Virgin Films, who in anticipation of making an Anglo-Italian production, found an Italian 'action' director in Sergio Corbucci. As Ned Sherrin amusingly relates in his autobiographical memoir* '*The Bodyguard Man* excited him, football excited him, the faint hint that "Giorgio Best" might play the footballer – lots of action, few lines – excited him; but as our meetings became more serious he began to have great doubts about the story. The characters were perfect, the plot was perfect, the action sequences were perfect. The trouble was that they were Italian. No Italian would believe that Italians would behave like our characters. Now, if we were to set our piece in Spain, everybody would believe that Spaniards would behave like that – except possibly some Spaniards: but this was not important.' This observation was curiously prescient, since in March 1981 a leading Spanish player was kidnapped and held to ransom for several weeks before

* *A Small Thing – Like an Earthquake* (Weidenfeld & Nicolson)

being released, but plans for the making of the film of **THE BODYGUARD MAN**, despite trips to Rome, to Madrid and to Los Angeles, eventually foundered through lack of investment.

When my third novel, **PLAYING THE WILD CARD**, was published in 1988, it came as further testament to my continuing long-distance obsession with Fiorentina. During the intervening fifteen years, however, much had changed inside the Italian game. 1980 proved a crucial year that witnessed a major scandal concerning the betting on League matches during the previous season, when over a score of players were found guilty of 'fixing' games, including Paolo Rossi, who found glorious form after two years of suspension to become the leading goalscorer in the Italian team in the 1982 World Cup. 1980 also saw the reopening of its doors to foreign players, which had been closed in 1965. If John Charles of Wales was highly-revered in the late Fifties, then Liam Brady of Eire, Trevor Francis and Ray Wilkins of England along with Graeme Souness of Scotland have been recent participants in Italian football whose skills were much admired – with Brady one of the foreign players who has survived longest in the cauldron which sees football treated with all the passion and intensity of a religion. In the match I saw there were only two imported players on view, but as the number of foreigners permitted to play for any club rose to two in 1982 and to three in 1988, football in Italy has become a veritable Mecca for imported stars – and increasingly so since 1988 when the number of clubs in the *Serie A* was increased from 16 to 18.

Although I've made certain changes, I decided not to update the novel in this regard. The reintroduction of foreign players and the custom of paying many of them enormous wages means that Italian football needs to promote itself more strenuously than before, particularly after that triumph in the World Cup in 1982. The influential sporting press is often swift to criticise and slow to praise, but for many, living and playing in Italy, with all the prestige and glamour involved, can be the most rich and stimulating experience, and many are paid most handsomely.

However, if celebrated imported stars such as Paolo Roberto Falcao, Michel Platini, Karl-Heinz Rummenigge and Zico in the past and Diego Maradona and Ruud Gullit in the present have been paid salaries that are truly phenomenal, leading home-reared players such as Franco Baresi, Gianluca Vialli and Roberto Baggio who experience similar pressure are looked after almost as generously. Although the playing fortunes of Fiorentina and Cagliari have fallen in the past twenty years, the essentially 'Italian' theme of the book remains perfectly plausible; and although the Stadio Communale, with its celebrated cantilever stand, has recently been renovated to host four games in the 1990 World Cup, it still retains the elegant structure it had twenty-one years ago when I first became fascinated by Fiorentina, '*la squadra del mio cuore*'.

Philip Evans, February 1990

PROLOGUE

TRANSCRIPT OF INTERVIEW dated 5th January, 1987.

PRESENT: Detective Sergeant Sam Langley
              Chief Inspector Simon Ricketts
              Commander David Bennetts
Special Branch   (Section 'C')

Timed at 10.36 a.m.

RICKETTS: We can take the hotel incident as read, Sergeant. What did you do once you'd discovered that Sudkovitch was no longer there?

LANGLEY: Well, sir, we decided that he wasn't likely to return and made our way down to the docks.

RICKETTS: Time, Sergeant?

LANGLEY: Ten to seven, sir. We made for the harbour-master's office just in case they had any further information on shipping movements.

RICKETTS: And?

LANGLEY: They had, sir. There was this Polish trawler, the *Grdzde*, that had just come in with engine trouble. It was berthed up to the north of the east point, just south of Harwich navy yard. We went up there fairly quick, if you know what I mean, sir. Just in case Sudkovitch was going to be very silly and make a run for it early before all the staff had packed it in for the evening.

RICKETTS: And you waited till when?

LANGLEY: Eleven twenty-seven by my watch, sir. Sure

enough, the customs people went off duty, and the offices began closing down. There were one or two lights on, but no real life.

RICKETTS: And you saw Sudkovitch, first, Sergeant? Or Harry Mann?

LANGLEY: Harry, sir. He was standing in a gap between two low offices, across the concrete walk from me, say fifty yards away. Of course there was some light, not a lot, but enough for us to see each other by. I saw him move his hand and point up the quay, so I poked my head out and took a peek. Sudkovitch was standing close to the customs shed, and I looked back and there was a gun in his hand, Harry's I mean.

RICKETTS: One moment, Sergeant. The gun Harry was carrying was what?

(Pause)

LANGLEY: A Beretta, sir. Calibred point-three-two.

RICKETTS: Not, then, the regulation firearm.

LANGLEY: Well. (Pause.) You know him, sir, he's so good with those things perhaps he likes to choose what suits him best.

RICKETTS: Never mind. Go on.

LANGLEY: Well, the Inspector's out and running before I have time to think. And then all hell breaks loose. A couple of characters come down the gang-plank of the ship and start popping shots off at him, and Sudkovitch is making for the boat as fast as he can, so I decide to join in the fun. I zigzag across the quay until I'm up with Harry and then Sudkovitch goes down. He's slipped just short of the gang-plank and he's trying to put himself together again. He's a plum target so I look at Harry to see why he hasn't winged him and his gun's pointing straight at the floor. I get all set to hit Sudkovitch and then Harry's arm shoots out and knocks the gun from my hand. I open my mouth to yell at him and he just tells me to shut up and now his gun's pointing at me. (Pause.) Well, we stay like that for a few moments and Sudkovitch is on the boat and we watch a couple of sailors come down and cast off the ropes and that's that as far as the two of us are concerned.

RICKETTS: Your orders were simple, were they not, Sergeant.

LANGLEY: Yes, sir. To prevent subject from escape, to apprehend him wherever he may be found.

RICKETTS: So Harry Mann was not only carrying a gun that was unregistered. He forcibly prevented you from carrying out your duty?

(Pause)

LANGLEY: Well, sir, if you put it like that.

RICKETTS: Damn and blast him to hell.

BENNETTS: Simon!

RICKETTS: Sorry. All right, Sergeant, I want a written report from you on this episode as quickly as possible. You'll stay in this room until it's been completed.

LANGLEY: Yes, sir.

RICKETTS: And no white-washing, Sergeant. Just the facts.

Interview ended at 10.53 a.m.

1

As a piece of tailing it was a complete nonsense.

I spotted the car the moment I stepped through the single revolving door of the Hotel Excelsior Italie, possibly the most prestigious of Florence's many hotels. It was a light-coloured Volvo 740GL with a burly chauffeur behind the controls and two greyish shapes nestling above the rear seats. The chauffeur was staring too intently in the direction of the hotel and his was the only car parked in that confine of the Piazza Ognisanti that wasn't empty.

I edged towards the potted palm to one side of the doorway and wrapped my right hand more tightly around the butt of the gun where it snuggled in my coat pocket. The collar of the coat was turned up in protest against the chilly dampness of the night air, and that only served to make me more suspicious. Working at night had never been anyone's idea of fun. Working in rain and at night – that was obviously less funny. Too much of an accent on chance. And what bodyguard ever cared to admit that word into his vocabulary.

They weren't good, the men in the car. Hell, even a child raised on Saturday matinée soap-operas at the local cinema knows the golden rule about tailing work. Of course, there are the fancy ones about staying on the other side of the street and keeping your distances right and never showing your face. But the key to the thing is that of acting at all times in a manner as normal as possible.

Perhaps I'd stood there for a couple of seconds before I

became certain. The chauffeur had compounded his original mistake of over-interest by reaching far too quickly for the Volvo's starter-control. That made them strictly amateur and the muscles in my right hand more relaxed.

I still had no clear idea of their game. But it was their petrol, and I could only string them along. I turned left out of the hotel forecourt, left out of the piazza and set off eastwards along the Lungarno Amerigo Vespucci, part of the northern bank of Florence's famous river Arno.

Along the Vespucci (where else?) was the Florentine version of Harry's Bar: ground-floor, a lot of glass, net curtains, quiet that particular evening. I stopped in the doorway of Harry's, dug round in my pockets until I found cigarettes and lighter and fired one of the former. I stood there, back to the door and turned slowly. The evening traffic was thick, with sudden braking and klaxon noise as some of the city's worthies made for home and Mamma and the pasta. And there was the Volvo, trying its damnedest to squeeze into a gap in the row of parked cars on my side of the road.

The moment it had come to rest, the chauffeur's face a mask of anxiety, two pale blobs thrusting forward from the rear of the car to peer out in my direction, then I set out again, leaving behind the sounds of braking tyres, horns and exasperated cries of fellow-drivers as the Volvo rudely attempted to cut back into the traffic.

Bodyguard work involves mental and physical agility, a thorough grounding in the techniques and usages of sundry dangerous weapons, but above all it calls for immediate mastery of detail. Such details have to be assimilated swiftly, remembered accurately. A memory-block, a casual slip, bad information — so often it is these rather than inadequacy that makes life seem mean. And long experience of travelling between, and working within, the larger cities of Western Europe had taught me to teach myself as much as possible about one-way traffic systems and their importance.

Florence has got style and character. But at the moment I was more interested in the fact that it is a neat example of a city whose architectural beauties have been near-sabotaged by the most notorious by-product of the internal combustion engine and now seems determined to exact a mild form of retribution from its torturer. Much of the city-centre is a maze of one-way streets, and the ruling has been made to apply along stretches close to the Arno. Generally speaking, upon the northern bank you are forced to travel eastwards; along the southern bank you travel westwards; and, the pedestrian-bound Ponte Vecchio apart, you cross the river where you can.

The fact gave me the opportunity to create the time I needed. The boys in the car behind, they wanted to talk, and didn't know how to make their first move. A communications gap between desire and actuality. And that gave me the venue and the choice of timing.

Instead of crossing the first bridge I came to, the Ponte alla Carraia, I moved further along the riverbank, turned right, or southwards, across the Ponte Santa Trinita and slid into the one-way street that exited south. There I watched as the Volvo powered into life, screamed round the corner leading off the bridge to the north and disappeared swiftly behind an apartment-block, the chauffeur desperately trying to cover as speedily as possible the three sides of the rectangle my move had forced him to negotiate. They didn't even do the obvious – put someone down to follow me on foot.

All that hanky-panky gave me time to make my way leisurely towards the Piazza Santo Spirito; to a small trattoria in the south-west corner at which I had often eaten during previous visits to Florence.

And it was there that they found me half an hour later.

2

ONLY TWO OF them came in, the men I had not yet clearly seen, and they made a stark contrast as to size, shape and accoutrement. One I recognised instantly from having seen his likeness in Italian daily newspapers and weekly gossip journals. The other's face was new to me.

Tozzi was the name of the man I recognised, Dino Tozzi. His photograph was an ever-present on the sports pages of the more prestigious Italian papers by virtue of the fact that he had for several years been employed as coach to the local football team, AC Fiorentina. I placed his age in the region of the mid-forties, perhaps slightly younger, but certainly not as young as myself. He was slim in build, medium in height, with bright bird-brown eyes and greying crinkled hair whose style would have aroused the admiration of a Roman senator. He was dressed casually in a burgundy polo-neck sweater, tan jacket, light-grey slacks. He seemed the sort of man who would look casual whatever he chose to wear. His comments in the press had always suggested a rounded personality, brimming with resource and a talent for the laconic phrase in moments of difficulty. Now he looked decidedly worried, the lines at the edges of his eyes wrinkled in apprehension. But he never looked as worried as his companion.

The character with Tozzi was a large-boned, well-girthed smoothie dressed in an expensive midnight-blue lightweight. White shirt, dark-patterned tie, both silken to the eye. He was dabbing athletically at a large expanse of sepia-coloured forehead with a bandana large enough to

19

make sheets out of. The forehead closed off a fleshy face, wide at nostril, mouth, across cheekbones. In contrast to Tozzi he looked the type of man for whom movement of even the apologetic kind would prove a strain. And dressed in that ensemble, given that locale, he looked as out of place as a new Ferrari at a used-car sale.

It's a popular restaurant, the Oreste, it was nearly fully subscribed that evening, and it took Tozzi and his companion some time to locate me. Once they had made the connection, ducked out through the hanging strips of plastic that fringed the doorframe, reappeared again a few seconds later. No doubt an instruction of some sort had been delivered to the chauffeur of the Volvo.

I lifted the carafe of red wine in front of me and poured some into my glass just at the moment in which the two men reached my table.

'Signor Mann?' It was Tozzi who had spoken.

I nodded.

'My name is Tozzi, Dino Tozzi. This is Commendatore Giorgio Belmonte. May we join you?' A softish voice that enunciated the words clearly.

I waved a hand in the direction of the other chairs at the table. '*Prego*, Signor Tozzi.'

They settled themselves into two hard-backed, plastic-seated chairs. Belmonte looked decidedly damp and uncomfortable, on both counts more than I thought he had any right to be.

I caught Falsatti Oreste's eye, waited for him to come over, asked for two more glasses for my two new-found companions, but he didn't really have to be asked. On my way in earlier I had noticed the fact that a large picture of Tozzi was on the wall behind the bar in a smudgy four-colour print torn from a sporting magazine and depicting manager and first-team pool from the local football club. That was one man who knew what to do when given the chance of being placed close to a hero-figure. Two extra

20

glasses arrived swiftly in the tablecloth, propelled there by a large brown hand at the end of a bar-towel.

I poured wine into the glasses and Belmonte made a strange whining sound. I'm exaggerating, of course, but only slightly. I had disliked Belmonte on sight, and the consequence was that whatever he had done I would have been prepared to be denigratory about it. In fact it was a voice that was medium in pitch, but one, in that moment, that had to it an unpleasant wheedling sound.

'Dino, Dino,' Belmonte was saying. His face wore a warmly quizzical expression. 'We agreed that I was the one who should do the talking, no?'

A flicker of impatience crossed Tozzi's eyes. 'You're right,' he said quickly.

'Dino, I understand your concern,' Belmonte went on, 'but please allow me to handle this affair in the manner I see as being most suitable.'

'Yes, yes,' Tozzi murmured tightly. His eyes flicked towards mine. 'But let's get the thing moving.'

Belmonte spread his damp hands wide. 'Dino,' he said again, his voice heavy with reproach. He took his hands away, laid them on the table-top, turned soft dark-brown eyes on my face. He jerked a look over each shoulder, bent his head across the table towards mine. If he was trying to be secretive about something, he was going about it the wrong way. Everything about his manner was as subtle as the colouring on a supermarket beachball.

'Your name has been given to us, Signor Mann,' he said, 'your name has been given to us as being that of the best in your line of work. *E vero*, no?' He was speaking in a stage whisper that could have been heard in the piazza outside.

I didn't say anything. There was nothing for me to say. That kind of talk was not of my world.

'You see, Signor Mann,' Belmonte continued, still hunched massively across the table-top, 'we have a problem. Or rather it is that we may have a problem and we have been told, signor, that you may be able to aid us in trying to solve it.'

I glanced across at Tozzi. He was breaking and rebreaking pairs of rough wooden toothpicks, taking them out of the cruet-holder, snapping them with a quick jerk of the wrists. A small pile of miniature wooden logs had risen in front of him. He gave off an overwhelming impression of impatience.

Belmonte turned towards him also. 'Now that we are here, now that we have had an opportunity to see Signor Mann for ourselves, Dino, now I am more than ever convinced that he is the man to help us. You agree, Dino?'

Tozzi nodded unhappily. 'Of course, of course,' he murmured tightly.

Belmonte laid a well-manicured fingertip on the edge of my right hand. I took my hand away. His stayed where it was. 'Your name, Signor Mann, was given to us by Giovanni Regalia.'

That got me interested, but I was damned if I was about to let Belmonte see my interest. From earlier days I remembered that Regalia was one of the best policemen in Italy, a member of the *Nuoleo Investigativo*, the plain-clothes high-power branch of the local *carabiniere* force here in Central Tuscany.

Belmonte began speaking again. 'Regalia said that if we wanted protection, you were the man to come to. He said – ' But I cut him off.

For me, that sentence had been the final straw. And I didn't have to push my face across the table for my eyes to be only two feet away from those of Belmonte. 'I'd like to talk to Tozzi,' I said. 'And alone. My guess is that he is the man who knows what to say best, that you are the man with the sensibility of a moron but a wallet thick with large-denomination banknotes. Maybe later, Belmonte, if Tozzi and I make a deal, then we'll call you and talk money. For now, just leave us alone. So why don't you just take a walk in the piazza while Tozzi and I discuss this affair between ourselves. Just the two of us.'

I thought Belmonte would have a fit. The sepia of his skin darkened violently into a rose-wood colouring, appeared to become more damp than it had been at the moment in which he had entered the restaurant.

'I think we should listen to the Englishman, Giorgio,' Tozzi said. His voice was quiet and precise, but a long way from blind toadying. 'This is no time to become involved in wrangles as to who shall and who shall not attempt to recruit Signor Mann into our employment. We have been told that he is the best at his line of work, and we have been given the information by the best possible sources. Signor Mann's qualifications appear unimpeachable.' He shrugged. 'In that case, we are in his hands, surely?'

Belmonte had been staring wildly at him. Suddenly he nodded his large head, placed his hands at the edge of the table, pushed himself up. He rolled off among the tables, barely managing to make the door without cannoning into one of them.

'I'm sorry about that, Tozzi,' I said. 'But everything about him smelt rotten. All that business with the car. That struck me as being the sort of thing Belmonte would think up. Am I right?'

He smiled. 'Crazy, wasn't it? But useful for me to see you at work. You kept your head well, and I was really impressed by the way you eventually gave us the slip. You been to Florence a lot previously, or no?'

I nodded. 'Enough. But remember it's all part of the work. It's always best to know where you're going in case you ever have to get there. But look at Belmonte. *Un disastro.* If there's one thing that we people hate it is having to discuss things in public. Waiters, maids, toilet attendants, parking-meter officials – they all have ears, they're all easy to bribe. If Belmonte really had something to say to me, he should have said it in his own time, at a private place of his choosing. A few more seconds of Belmonte and the whole damned restaurant would have known what he didn't want the whole damned world to know.'

Tozzi held a hand up. 'Let's start again, Signor Mann. You may know that I am coach to the local football team?'

I nodded.

'Then you will have guessed that Giorgio Belmonte is involved with the club in a financial capacity.'

'I don't see him as being the club president,' I said. 'From what I have read of the game in Italy club presidents strike me as being the most urbane of the species.'

'You're right, of course. He isn't president, vice-president or secretary. But he does control a fair percentage of the share holding, and he is undoubtedly the wealthiest member among the Fiorentina board of directors.'

'So how does he come into this particular picture?' I asked.

'As you have pointed out this is no time to discuss the affair in detail. Let me just say that over a period of three weeks my best player has received a series of letters threatening his life. For reasons that I am not prepared to elaborate now, we have reached a position in which we must take these threats very seriously.'

'And Belmonte?' I asked.

'He pressed himself upon me in the matter. The player concerned is wealthy, his valuation on the transfer market is close to 3 million of your pounds sterling, Signor Mann. On both counts Belmonte felt himself intimately involved in the affair. And he is not an easy man to deny.'

'That doesn't mean that you think much of him, does it, Tozzi?' I asked.

He didn't reply.

'I understand your reticence to discuss the relationship,' I said.

'You haven't yet given us any indication as to whether you are prepared to take the enquiry any further, Mann,' Tozzi said. His voice was slightly stiff.

I nodded. 'All right. Don't get upset about it on my

account. You must be upset enough already. I plan to stay in Florence for a couple of days, visiting friends. Just give me a time, a place for a meeting and I'll be there.'

'What of money?'

I shook my head. 'Money won't buy me, Tozzi. Certainly, I'll want paying and paying well. But only if the job appeals to me. I've been in this game too long not to know that an acceptance of work motivated merely by the greed for money can prove fatal.'

Tozzi nodded, handed over a piece of card with the football club's address written thereon: 'AC Fiorentina, Viale Manfredo Fanti 4/6 – Viale dei Mille 66'.

'Come to the second address,' Tozzi said. 'What time?'

'Midday?' I asked.

He nodded, shook hands, then pushed his chair back preparatory to leaving. And that was when I stopped him.

'One moment,' I said. 'I'd like to tell you a story.'

He looked puzzled, but pulled his chair in again.

'It was in Turin, a couple of years ago,' I explained. 'I speak Italian fluently and consequently find myself being offered jobs here in large proportion. I was doing some gentle babysitting at a convention of automobile salesmen drawn from most of the Western European countries. All very civilised, but naturally the civility was largely a veneer. Only a few moments in the company of these people would have taught a cretin that. The polarisation was evident in almost everything that took place, with certain factions staying away from, and nastily eyeing, each other.

'At seven one morning I was called on the house telephone and ordered by a shrill, hysterical voice to come down to the third floor. Which I did. And it wasn't too pleasant.' I paused to make sure of his attention. He was staring at me with puzzled eyes that also betrayed worry. 'He was in his early thirties, a good-looking fellow slightly gone to seed. He seemed to be asleep, lying in the bed on his right side. In the room was a maid, the hotel manager and one of the organising delegates to the convention. Rigor mortis had already begun to rigidify the cells. I ordered the others away and looked him over for flaws, and guess what I found? Just visible inside one ear was a piece of metal the size of a small blob of mercury.'

'What was it, this thing?' Tozzi asked quietly. He was paler than he had been moments before.

'A knitting needle,' I said, 'cut in half and filed to a wicked point. Some cute bastard had known exactly what he was doing, someone with a lot of verve and finesse. A professional killing. So I asked a few questions and established the identity of the dead man as a French operator who had been fiddling some very lucrative contracts on the side. And contracts was the right word. This was a contract killing, a perfect job executed by a real professional on the behalf of one of the other delegates.'

'What is the real point of your story?' Tozzi said in a breathy whisper.

'Just this,' I said. I pointed my right forefinger at him. 'I'm not going to threaten you, but you may do well to listen to this piece of advice. You don't yet know, and I don't yet know, whether there is a problem here and whether I'm going to be involved in it. But if I am, and you think you can trust me, you'd be a damn fool to cover anything up, however trivial it may seem to you. If I give you a footballing analogy, you may grasp the point more clearly. The other team has the ball, so what do you do? You use your experience and your knowledge of their patterns of play to get into good positions. So with this game. The bodyguard or whoever is always in a defensive position, always one move behind. And if the information he has to work with is opaque or erroneous he's in dead trouble. If only someone at that convention in Turin had had the sense to warn me of what was going on, I might have got the Frenchman out of that town in one piece.'

'I see,' Tozzi said.

'It's important,' I warned. I shook his hand again. 'I'll see you tomorrow.'

He nodded, stood up, made his way to the door and left the restaurant. There was a tenseness in his walk that I hadn't noticed earlier in the evening.

3

I ROSE EARLY the next morning and went through my usual session of exercises. It's a young man's game, this one, and there are times when I feel too old. Ask Al Capone. Mention his torpedoes to most people and they conjure up mental sketches of middle-aged heavyweights who ate too much spaghetti and were mean with a Thompson 'type-writer'. Not so. The vast majority died in their twenties, and none of them died because they weren't physically honed to a fine edge of fitness.

I pulled out my knife and spent a few minutes sharpening the edges. It's a nice weapon if you like that sort of thing, a thin metal blade between two ivory slats and with a press-catch that flicks it open to an overall length of some eight inches. On the few occasions in which I'd used it, the natural resting-place had been beside my left ankle. A throwing-knife, and with the opportunity to find some sense of balance, I found it useful up to thirty or forty feet.

I tucked the knife away in my suitcase, showered, shaved, dressed and crossed the piazza.

The Chiesa Ognisanti was almost deserted for the early morning mass. There were one or two old ladies kneeling up among the front pews and the priest on duty didn't really sound as though he'd managed to wipe the sleep-dirt out of his eyes. I took a seat near the back and looked around. Scaffolding and bags of cement tended to give the real atmosphere. Yet another beautiful piece of architecture that had been ravaged by the flood-waters of November 1966.

The reedy voice of the priest grew stronger in proportion to his wakefulness, so that even the vileness of the Tuscan dialect was unable to spoil for me the meaning of the words he was chanting.

On the way out into the square I bought and lit a candle. A candle for the dead? That wasn't for me to say.

* * *

Noon found me exiting from a taxi opposite the club offices in the tree-lined, car-burdened width of the Viale dei Mille, the Way of the Thousands.

The offices were set on the first floor of a block of business flats propped up by a gun-shop and a miniature paradise for sailing exponents. The gun-shop stocked sporting rifles, not the sort people buy when they want to make a real nuisance of themselves apropos their fellow human beings.

Several people were waiting in the reception area of the AC Fiorentina offices, the majority seemingly involved in trying to extract gratis tickets for the next home match the following Sunday afternoon. A slim character in pink shirt, dark-blue tie and dark-brown suit was explaining patiently that the day was Tuesday, they'd have to wait until Thursday at the earliest to be sure of being allocated their places. Come back then, he said, and strode off into a cool office to one side. As though that was enough to deter his pursuers. They merely sank down into the comfortable chairs dotted around and awaited his next appearance.

The commissionaire was a middle-sized, middle-aged character wearing dark-blue blazer, hair pomade and club tie. His nose from the front looked like a collector's item – wide across the nostrils, pointed into a sharp tip, a pale Ace of Spades.

I waited to one side of his desk until he was ready to drag his eyes away from the cheapstream thriller he was reading.

'*Prego, signor,*' he said.

'*Sono qui per parlare con Tozzi,*' I said.

30

His voice hardened. '*Signor Tozzi?*'

I didn't reply, simply stared at him.

'*C'e?*' he asked gruffly.

'*C'e Il Inglese,*' I said.

He wasn't clever. He worked on that one until the right button pressed in his memory, then became obsequious. '*Si, signor. Subito.*' He stood up, inclined his head slightly, held an arm out. I followed him down the corridor.

Tozzi's office was half-way down the corridor on the left-hand, street side. His name was stencilled on to the glass sheeting of the door in violet, the colour in which the Fiorentina team played. I went in after the commissionaire.

Tozzi wasn't alone. And many things clicked into place in my memory.

The man sitting in the lounge chair to one side of Tozzi's desk looked long, slim, wiry, about forty years of age, and strikingly handsome. His hair was thick and dark, his features regular, his small ears lay close to his skull. He was wearing a tan suit, white shirt, plain dark-blue tie, black shoes with a rim that curled round the instep into a buckle.

He stood up from the chair once the commissionaire had gone and shook hands warily, without waiting for the introduction that would have been unnecessary.

This was Giovanni Regalia, the man that Belmonte had mentioned to me the previous evening before I had silenced him. I had met many Italian policeman in that time; I couldn't remember one who stood within hailing distance of Regalia when it came to negotiating a way through a tricky case.

'I thought you'd be interested,' he said. The loose baritone voice went well with the relaxed attentiveness of his eyes.

I shrugged. 'I thought you thought I'd be interested,' I said. 'Belmonte mentioned your name yesterday evening. That meant that something interesting was in the air.'

We stared at each other warily. Then Tozzi came

forward, shook hands, offered me a chair. I took it, moved it over to the door so that I could see both of them without having to strain the muscles of my neck. Regalia was a good man to keep in one's sights.

No-one seemed very eager to do any talking. Tozzi was fiddling with some papers on his desk, Regalia was staring off into the middle distance above the top of my head. I pulled my cigarettes out, lit one, looked round for an ashtray. There was an ashtray perched on the edge of Tozzi's desk. I reached for it, and that was when I saw the one edge of the paper he had been trying to shuffle out of sight.

I eased it out, saw that it was a tan-coloured envelope. In the centre were the words RESOCONTO PRIVATO. A confidential report, and there in the top right-hand corner was my surname, written in the same thick-nibbed printing.

Neither Regalia nor Tozzi said or did anything as I unwound the loop of string from its holder at the back, drew out the large card therein and began to read it. The greater part of the information it contained had been typed out. Just a handful of holograph insertions at various points. This is what I read:

Name: MANN
Given Names: HAROLD (HARRY) JAMES
Date of Birth: 26th JULY, 1956
Place of Birth: CANTERBURY, ENGLAND
Nationality: BRITISH (Holograph addition: Also known (one occasion) operating under name of LACLOS, GEORGES; French papers)
Passport No: 562918
Height: 6 FEET 1 INCH (185 cms)
Weight: 13 STONES 5 POUNDS/LBS (85 kilos)
Country of Residence: NOMINALLY BRITAIN (BUT SEE BELOW)
Only known Address: 3 BRUNSWICK MANSIONS, HANDEL STREET, LONDON, WC1 (RENTED 4-ROOMED APARTMENT)
Marital Status: CELIBATE, CELIBE

Colour of Eyes: BLUE/GREY

Colour of Hair: BLACK

Special Distinguishing Marks: (*a*) SCARS (1) SHORT ONE-INCH (2.5 cms) SCAR POINT OF JAW, (2) SIX-INCH (15 cms) SCAR FROM ELBOW TO WRIST ON RIGHT ARM (OUTSIDE), (3) CIRCULAR SCAR, CIRCA ONE-INCH (2.5 cms) ABOVE 7th VERTEBRA ON BACK (*b*) SMALL BIRTHMARK LEFT TRICEP

Relatives: FATHER (ALEXANDER), MOTHER (LOUISE) BOTH DECEASED. NO OTHER RELATIVES

Special Interests: NONE RECORDED

Special Habits: (*a*) SMOKES OCCASIONALLY — CIGARETTES, BENSON AND HEDGES FILTER TIPS (*b*) DRINKS VERMOUTH, GIN — AGAIN OCCASIONALLY (*c*) KNOWN TO GAMBLE TO MODERATION

Special Training: TRAINED TO EXPERTISE IN USE OF (*a*) RIFLE (*b*) HAND-GUN (*c*) THROWING KNIFE (*d*) CUTTING KNIFE. NO RECORDED KNOWLEDGE OF JUDO, KARATE, AIKIDO BEYOND USE OF BASIC TENETS

Political Attitudes: NO KNOWN STANDS TO EXTREMES OF LEFT OR RIGHT

Brief History: NINE-EIGHT-SEVENTY-FOUR — BRITISH ARMY (MILITARY SERVICE). EIGHT-TWELVE-SAME — SECOND LIEU-TENANT BRITISH ARMY EDUCATION CORPS. SEVEN ELEVEN-SEVENTY-SIX — CONSTABLE METROPOLITAN POLICE FORCE (LONDON — WEST END CENTRAL STATION). ELEVEN-SEVEN SEVENTY-NINE SELECTED FOR TRAINING POLICE COLLEGE BRAMSHILL (nr. BASINGSTOKE). FIVE-SEVEN-EIGHTY REC-OMMENDED TO JOIN SPECIAL BRANCH SECTION DEPARTMENT 'C' METROPOLITAN POLICE, THREE-FOUR-EIGHTY-ONE — APPOINTED DETECTIVE SERGEANT SPECIAL BRANCH. TWENTY/SEVEN-ELEVEN-EIGHTY-THREE — APPOINTED DETECTIVE INSPECTOR SPECIAL BRANCH. EIGHTEEN-ONE-EIGHTY SEVEN — RESIGNED. AT PRESENT FREELANCE BODY-GUARD OPERATING WESTERN EUROPE.

Record of Linguistics: ENGLISH, ITALIAN, FRENCH: ALL FLUENT. WORKING KNOWLEDGE GERMAN, SPANISH

Comments: (i) MANN HAS OPERATED IN THE FOLLOWING WEST-
ERN EUROPEAN CITIES SINCE SPRING ONE-NINE-EIGHTY-
SEVEN: MADRID, PARIS, ATHENS, VIENNA, MARSEILLES,
AMSTERDAM, MUNICH, GENEVA, TURIN, ZURICH, MILAN,
LONDON, ROME, COPENHAGEN, BONN (SEE APPENDICES
i–xlv)
(ii) REASONS FOR LEAVING SPECIAL BRANCH NEVER MADE
CLEAR. INCOMPATABILITY (?): REPORTS OF WORK DURING
LAST FOUR YEARS HINT AT THIS
(iii) SEEMINGLY EXCELLENT PHYSICAL QUALIFICATIONS
(iv) AN OPERATOR OF SOME RESOURCE AND INTELLIGENCE
(v) COMPARE FILES OF *De Vriete; Mannen; Lasalle; Dubois;
Kriestien:; Odermann* (ALL CODED SECTION Ex2)

I replaced the card in the envelope, returned the envelope
to the top of Tozzi's desk.

'We were discussing all this when you arrived,' Regalia
said.

'Fine,' I said. 'Don't mind me. I'm not here. You just
carry on.'

Regalia scowled. His eyes never left my face, but he
resumed his conversation with Tozzi. 'You get the picture,
Signor Tozzi. Mann is one of a small handful of men who
hire themselves out as bodyguards. You hear the word
bodyguard and you think of ex-boxers with broken noses,
too much aggression, no tact. Don't make that mistake.
Mann is not of that breed but of a world that is strictly
professional. If he is not the best man in Europe – and it
may well be that he is – then he is certainly among the first
two or three. The Frenchman, Lasalle, the German, Odermann, rate highly along with him. The former is undoubtedly a better technician than Mann but tends to be over-
excitable: the latter very thorough but never quite resource-
ful enough – too stolid, perhaps. As a compromise, then,
Mann is the best.'

'Go on, Regalia,' I said. 'Tell Tozzi about the other file

you've got, you probably code it *Section EX1*. Let's get the picture absolutely straight.'

I looked at Tozzi and sensed his bewilderment. He knew he was caught in an intricate game of words and attitudes. He also knew that the time was a good one in which to keep silent, to stay on the banks of the river.

'Tell him about Darouche,' I said to Regalia. 'And Korlensky. And Mueller. And Dorpmanns. And dear lovable Mohammed Benkaddour, the friendly Moroccan who's never happy unless the tang of cordite is in the air. Tell him about them, then he might get a clear picture and stop thinking of me as a hired killer.'

Regalia was still staring at me. 'The names Mann has mentioned are those of the most expensive killers in Europe, the men who charge enormous fees and tackle seemingly impossible tasks. Their number was greater by three a few years ago, until Mann came into the picture. All he is trying to point out is the difference between himself and these men. They are the dragons; he set himself up as St George, with his shining suit of armour and his trusty lance.'

I could feel the muscles in my fingers and wrists tauten. 'I've never killed anyone, Regalia,' I said. 'And you know that. I was nearby when the plane exploded with Perez inside; I was nearby when Wolff was gunned down; I was nearby when the car carrying Zwemmer crashed. But I didn't kill any of them and your files will prove me right.'

'It isn't relevant,' Regalia said. 'Maybe you professional bodyguards don't have the sadistic streak or the urge to kill, but you have everything else – the arrogance, the almost childlike fascination in action for the sake of action, the perpetual need to satisfy your egos, the vanity.' He pointed a lean forefinger at me, but turned towards Tozzi. 'He used to work for the Special Branch, no? Hell, I can tell you all about them. A real collection of elitists, those boys. They wouldn't be seen dead having a drink with the CID, let alone the uniform branch. They have a bar in the

35

basement of the New Scotland Yard building in London. They call it the "Tank", and the last time a Special Branch man was seen there was never. Vain bastards.' He paused. 'And that's Mann's background for you.'

I scowled at him. 'Bullshit, Regalia. You recommended me to Tozzi, you've given me your little sermon. I know what the sermon was for. That was just to let me know that you think you've got me properly weighed up. Maybe you have. It's not important. What *is* important is this problem concerning Corrente. That's what's important.'

Even Regalia looked shaken at that. As for Tozzi he just looked shattered.

4

'How DID YOU know it was him?' Regalia asked darkly.

'Come on,' I said. 'Just for a few moments tuck away that suspicious nature of yours. You think I went back to my hotel and went straight to sleep? Don't be ingenuous. First I made two phone-calls to Milan and Rome, nice chatty phone-calls to friends who knew something about football. They got round to Corrente soon enough once I had mentioned the fact that I was in Florence. There didn't seem to be anyone else in the Fiorentina squad they were interested in. That gave me the player's name. So then I wandered down to the reception area in the Hotel Excelsior and got one of the boys there to dig up as many old papers as he could find. I talked to him about football. He thought I was perhaps a commercial traveller, a journalist, a man who liked talking and listening. He talked, I listened. And when he went away I read the material he'd brought with him. I found it interesting. And the obvious point struck me immediately.'

'Which was?' Regalia said.

'That in the interviews he gave before or after a match Tozzi usually referred to his players by their surnames. Corrente, no. It was always "Gianni this" or "Gianni that". And the match reports confirmed everything I've heard and read. He's the star of the team. Without him, they play well but without clarity. The brain of the outfit, Corrente, no?' I turned to Tozzi. '*Il cervello.*'

He nodded.

'Which all kept me busy this morning,' I went on. I

reached for my wallet, pulled out a slip of paper. 'This is what I've gathered. *Corrente, Gianni* was born 2.4.67 in Cagliari, Sardinia. Grew up there, played schools, then local club football. Aged fifteen he was spotted by someone from AC Cagliari and signed on to the club's books. Three summers later AC Fiorentina paid the vast sum of a thousand lire for him, that was the summer of 1983, when he was 18. He goes straight into the Fiorentina first team, and within months of joining Fiorentina he wins his first national cap. Now he has established a regular place in the Italian side. And just you guess who has been Fiorentina's manager for the past few years.' I looked up at Tozzi.

He blinked quickly. 'I could have told you all that,' he said.

'Surely you could,' I said. 'But that wasn't the point. Look, Tozzi, bodyguard work is comparable to all walks of life in this respect. Unless you've done your homework, you're always groping in the dark. So I did some homework. Not much, I admit, but enough. Now I know what you're going to be talking about. See.' I grinned at him to give him reassurance.

He smiled.

'Now that you two are getting pally with each other,' Regalia growled, 'let's move on to the question of Corrente's safety.' He stood up, pulled an envelope out of the inside breast-pocket of his suit. 'Look at that,' he said to me, handing it over. I took it carefully.

It was a plain white envelope, not lined in the interior as many Continental envelopes are. The postmark read *Poste Firenze Ferr. Corrisp.* with the date, that of the previous Saturday. The writing on the envelope was in roll-nib, printed in gawky capitals, addressed to Tozzi at the stadium address, rather than at the office.

No initials or Christian names. Just the "TOZZI".

I looked up at Regalia. He nodded his permission so I slid out the piece of paper that was inside and held the envelope up against the light. The word *Superbianco* was watermarked on the face. No other markings, no smudges near the seal-line. Nothing.

There was a watermark on the stiffish sheet of white paper inside, a string of Japanese characters down one edge. And in the centre of the page, again printed in capitals, each word distinctly separate from its neighbour, was the message:

THREE TIMES WE HAVE WARNED CORRENTE. ON EACH OCCASION HE HAS CHOSEN TO IGNORE US. NOW WE WARN YOU. UNLESS CORRENTE IMMEDIATELY ACCEDES TO OUR DEMANDS, HE WILL BE FINISHED.

'*Sara finito*,' I said. 'But that doesn't mean that anyone will kill him.'

Regalia shook his head. 'I don't think so, but this,' he took back the paper and envelope, 'I take this seriously. And here's why.' He passed over another piece of paper for me to look at.

Again it was white, but this time the message was printed in crude upper and lower case Roman type. It was addressed at the top 'AI LAVORATORI E AI CITTA-DINI SARDO'. Beneath the address was the message urging the workers and citizens of Sardinia to attend mass rallies at the three largest towns on the island – Cagliari, Sassari and Nuoro – against mainland domination of the less fortunate *isole* and regions. Money for better roads, housing, schools, hospitals, that was the theme.

'For some time now,' Regalia said, 'movements such as this have grown in strength in the less wealthy parts of Italy: down in the south in Sicily, in Sardinia. This,' he pointed at the broadsheet, 'this is fairly typical in its language. The central government is a thief, and thieves must be made to give up what they have stolen. These people hold rallies, go on marches, picket the government offices in Rome. Of course, their claims have a certain validity. And equally obviously, these movements attract a hard core of extremists. Which is where Corrente comes in.' He stopped.

Tozzi took up the theme. 'It is important to remember that Gianni Corrente is a Sardinian boy. And equally important to get the game of football in Italy into a rightful perspective. Footballers here are paid very well, the top players take home tens of millions of lire a year. They are fêted by industrialists, spoilt by show-business acquaintances, praised by politicians, adored by the crowds. But the passions run high to both directions and away from the adoration of the fans, players are often vilified and insulted by the supporters of the other teams.

'Now the number of players from the two main islands – Sicily and Sardinia – who make good in the game is desperately small; a minute, very talented, handful. But the fact remains that their symbolic importance to a club is extreme. For instance, Juventus have a wonderfully talented Sicilian boy playing at centre-forward. A couple of seasons ago he played well below form and the club considered the possibility of transferring him during the summer market season. They didn't dare to do it. There are so many Sicilians working in and near Turin that the club almost became terrified of what would happen to their property.

'We don't have that kind of fanaticism here in Florence. But you and Regalia know about these things. You know that just a handful of these characters can cause a disproportionate amount of trouble. Gianni Corrente certainly feels it. Every time we travel to an away fixture there will be some members of the crowd, the transplanted Sardinians, who are there merely to watch him – often people not particularly interested in football, but who see the boy as a symbolic figure, the Sardinian who crossed the waters and beat the mainland people at their game and on their territory.' He stopped.

'And Corrente feels this pressure constantly?' I asked.

Tozzi nodded. 'Of course. Everywhere he goes people are forced into extremes of attitude.'

'But he hasn't mentioned this business of these threatening letters?'

'Not recently,' Regalia intervened. 'These people in Sardinia, the autonomy boys, held their first rally about four weeks ago. They got in touch with Corrente in an attempt to elicit his support. They wanted him to sign declarations, attend meetings, involve himself in marches, aim at exposure of this problem in the media. They were unsuccessful. You can see the point. Corrente knew well enough that an involvement of this nature might prejudice his game, he might lose form. Certainly he would excite an animosity among the mainlanders who think of the people from the islands as being un-Italian. *Non sono Italiani*, they will say of Sicilians and Sardinians. They are thought of by such people as having come from a lower plane of humanity.'

'Fantastic,' I said, to keep him talking.

Regalia shrugged. 'I agree, but don't ever think that the constitution of present-day Italy is little more than a mere papering-over of some very pronounced regional differences. No matter. Corrente was wise not to get involved. He was sensible enough to realise that he would merely be a pawn in the hands of the autonomists. You can turn in all the arguments about mixing politics and sport; and you can turn them around all the ways you want to. But it was not a clear-cut matter in Corrente's view. He decided to stay out.'

'And then came the first of the threatening letters?' I asked.

'Hell, it's difficult,' Regalia said. 'Players of this calibre often get abusive letters from bad-tempered supporters, fanatics, the crazy element. They don't take them seriously. If they're sensible, that is. But the letters to Corrente were more vicious, much more personal, several steps further on from the world of abusive language.'

41

'What did they say?' I asked. 'By the way, how many have there been?'

'To date, three. All posted in Florence, but all purporting to have come from Cagliari. All threatened in mild tones – "You are in real trouble, Corrente", "So you think you're too good for the people you left behind. Soon you'll see" – that kind of thing.'

'And Corrente handed these over to you?' I asked Tozzi.

He nodded, then shook his head. 'Yes. No. He came to me and talked about them when he received the second letter last Saturday. He told me of the attempts made to recruit him to the cause, asked my advice. I asked him for the notes. He wouldn't let me have them at first. I put pressure on him, tried to make him realise that perhaps they would be better off in my hands. As soon as I got them I passed them over to Regalia.'

'Tell him about Bologna,' Regalia said to Tozzi.

Tozzi nodded. 'Ten days ago we played at the Stadio Communale in Bologna. We played well. We won. The Bologna fans were angry. But there was something terror-inducing at the systematic way in which our team coach was stoned by the crowd. I've been in situations similar to that before, but never one which so scared me.'

Silence fell for a few moments.

I interrupted it. 'You see the problems from my point of view, Regalia?'

He nodded.

I turned to Tozzi. 'There's the primary problem of duality: Corrente is popular with Sardinians. Corrente is unpopular with Sardinians. Maybe it is true that a hard core of fanatics is keen to get at him. But are they really serious? Is one footballer, however famous his personality, however prestigious his possible support, worth the trouble that you suggest they are prepared to go to? Maybe, maybe not. It's a touch-and-go affair.

'There is another possibility; namely that the Sardinians' business is merely a smoke-screen put up by someone here in Florence. All these letters have been posted locally. Agreed the time factor may be important – all these letters have been received coincidentally to political participants on the part of Sardinian activists. But the link still leaves room for doubt. My guess is that Regalia has no fingerprint evidence worth speaking of apropos those letters. Too many prints to enable him to draw conclusions and have names. Am I right?'

Regalia nodded.

'Then there is Belmonte,' I said. 'Tell me, Tozzi, how many people inside the club know of these threats to Corrente's independence.'

Tozzi looked worried. 'That's the point, of course. As soon as this letter addressed to me arrived yesterday morning I rang Regalia. Of course I felt under compulsion to show it to the president and the directors. By no means all the directors saw it, but many did and Belmonte was one of those who came into the club's office as soon as he was informed of its nature. As the man with the most financial pull on the board he insisted upon complete involvement. Thus his presence yesterday evening.'

'He knows I'm here this morning?' I asked.

'I told him last night when I rejoined him in the car outside the trattoria.'

I nodded. 'Of course. But he hasn't seen that file on me that Regalia has produced?'

'That, no.'

'I don't want him to see it.'

'May I ask, Signor Mann,' Tozzi said, 'does this interest you've shown in this case indicate that you are prepared to consider the possibility of helping us?' It was a long, wordy way of getting to the point, a betrayal of Tozzi's anxiety.

'Of course I'm interested,' I said.

'And you can spare us how much time?'

'My next firm assignment is not until the end of the month. You think that will allow sufficient time?' I turned to Regalia.

He nodded. 'Maybe.'

'And the money?' Tozzi asked. 'This business is important to us, but we cannot afford to pretend that we have unlimited funds.'

'You have Belmonte,' I said.

Tozzi smiled. 'Of course. But after your treatment of him last night Belmonte is not disposed to view your personality in an over-favourable manner.'

'Let's agree this. Five hundred pounds, a hundred and fifty thousand lire a day, plus the use of a chauffeur-driven car and some money for expenses. We'll see how that goes for the time being.'

'You don't drive?' Tozzi asked incredulously.

'Explain to him, Regalia,' I said.

'Of course he can drive, Tozzi.' Regalia's voice was patient. 'But that's not the point. The point is that driving takes thought, use of hands and feet, concentration of the eyes. Mann is a specialist. So he knows that the fellow behind the wheel of a car is a sitting target, with no room to maneouvre, with all his faculties concentrated on keeping the car on the road. While he is driving a bodyguard ceases to be himself.' Regalia shrugged. 'So it all sounds very precious to you, no? But I should humour him. Give him a car and a man to drive the damn thing.'

Tozzi thought for a moment, then nodded briskly. 'That should be possible. Will you want an advance of money?'

'Could be,' I said. I stood up. 'There are still many details to be worked out. Perhaps if I can see you tomorrow morning?'

'Of course.'

'In the meantime, Tozzi, two things. First, send to my hotel everything you think important about Gianni Corrente's position within the club: list of directors, their occupations, notes about the back-room boys and the other players. That first. Second, I must have a free hand to do whatever I want. Just tell me this. Does Corrente know of the existence of the note you received yesterday morning?'

44

'Not to my knowledge.'

'He mustn't know, Tozzi,' I said grimly.

He nodded.

'I'll wait for the background material to arrive at the hotel, then ring you tomorrow morning,' I finished.

I looked in the direction of Regalia, made for the door. When I reached it I turned round.

'By the way, Tozzi,' I said. 'Next Sunday's match is what?'

'Against AC Milan.'

'Away?'

'Yes, at San Siro.'

'And the following Sunday?'

'At home against Roma.' Tozzi suddenly frowned. 'But on Wednesday we have to travel again to play the first leg of a quarter-final in the Coppa Italia against US Cagliari.'

I looked at him hard, nodded, went out of the door, along the corridor, through the reception area, down the stairs, and out into the street.

US Cagliari. Away.

In my position even a dimwit with a soup-strainer memory might have been able to remember that last piece of information to come from Tozzi's direction.

5

A HUNDRED METRES down the road I saw a bar with tables arranged outside, under an awning and surrounded by those thick clumps of boxed privet that are supposed to suggest to urban Italians something of the rich pleasures of the countryside.

I ordered a Riccadonna at the bar, went out and slid into a plastic-wrapped chair, seemingly well-hidden from a sighting down the road. But Regalia found me quickly enough. He spent a long time using his eyes and intelligence, say all of five seconds, then deciding to drop the act.

I watched him, lean and tall, all the way towards me. There are walks and walks; Regalia's walk was one I could admire, athletic and purposeful.

He nodded to me when he came close, went into the bar to order his drink, came back to the pavement, settled himself down in the chair across the metal-top table, made a great business of lighting a cigarette. I noticed that it was an imported German brand. I also noticed that it hadn't been sealed with the piece of sticky paper that the Italian customs place across all packets of imported cigarettes. Which all made Regalia nice and human. No doubt, like so many Italians, he was on the list of a *contrabandiere*, some murky character who would undertake to procure for him imported goods that hadn't undergone scrutiny from the officers in charge of customs and excise. It might even be worse: a member of the *Polizia di Frontiera*, perhaps?

I waited for the barman to bring out drinks, then made the point. 'Those,' I said, pointing at the cigarette packet.

'I'll wager they weren't brought in your friendly local tobacconist's.'

He coloured slightly. 'Very droll,' he said, with not a touch of amusement in his voice.

'Never mind,' I said. 'Seems you've got me a nice job, Regalia.'

'I hope you're worth the money,' he said.

'You know I am,' I replied. 'Whether I can do anything to help, I don't know. Perhaps at that there's only one way to find out. Ever heard of a case like this?'

He shook his head. 'Never. And I don't like it. Ninety-nine per cent of these threatening letter affairs are bluff, fake. This one smells to be like the real thing.' He held out a hand, turned it over, examined it carefully. 'But it's their money. They can do with it what they like.'

'So tell me,' I said, 'why you don't think these people are going after Corrente to kill or kidnap.'

He looked at me warily. 'I didn't say that.'

'That's what I mean. You didn't say anything. A lot of general information, yes. A lot of specific opinion, no. So now tell me what you really think.'

He made a big affair of mashing out his cigarette in the ashtray in front of him. He had barely touched it, the cigarette.

'I'll tell you about a dream I had. You interested?'

Whether I pretended interest or no, he would tell me. 'In everything you say and do, Regalia,' I growled, 'you're so fascinating.'

He stared at me sharply. '*Divertente*. Funny.' He lit up another of his contraband cigarettes, this time put the packet back into his coat pocket. 'You may not believe it, but it was *my* dream. So you listen, because I remember it distinctly. Imagine twenty years ago. I then played football for a local team. Good weekend games, all young men, all fit and enthusiastic. And like most weekend players the game for us was on the lines of a religion. Now,' he said slowly, 'now I know better. But it was then that I had my dream, a dream that took me to the top in football, brought me prestige and a vast sum of money. Me, a small-village boy, playing in front of enthusiastic, vociferous, adulatory crowds. It's true that Italy was not then as prosperous as it is now, that players earned only a fraction of the monies earned by their counterparts today. But wealth remains always relative, and the fame, the glory – they've been an ever-present in Italian football since the era of the *Fascist*, when Mussolini saw sporting victory as a fine means of propaganda and the Italian national team responded by winning the *Coppa Mondiale* twice in the space of four years. So far, routine storyline. So what happened in my dream? Everything was cut off from me, that's what happened. I was in a motorcycle crash; nothing serious except for the fact that all the bones in my right foot were crushed. You see the point?'

He was leaning across the table towards me. It was the first time I'd seen that earnest police look on his face, and it was as earnest a face as I had seen in a long time.

I nodded. 'So you think these characters – whoever they are – will try to pull something along these lines with Corrente?'

'Look at it this way, Mann,' Regalia said. 'It's a question of ratios. They kill the boy, even kidnap him, they'll get hell once they're caught. But a knife-slash across the tendons, they can't be put away for too long. The boy won't ever play football again perhaps, the crime is still vile in the context of the footballing world. But in the context of the *Codice Penale* it counts as next to nothing.'

'It's the easiest thing in the world to happen,' I said. 'And it doesn't have to be complicated.'

Regalia shrugged. '*Esatto*. So very easy. And it could come from the most unexpected source.'

We stared at each other for long seconds, very aware that the jealousy that existed between us had temporarily evaporated, had left us looking at cold hard facts with all the professionalism and training that we could command.

'It looks like the old journalist pose,' I said.

Regalia gave a tight smile. 'That one again.' His face fell back into its smooth mask. 'But you're right. And you see my problem. Tozzi doesn't want the boy's concentration upset, but this case requires someone to stay with the boy day and night, to act as his shadow. So say I put some of my men by his side, whatever the story I concoct someone will begin to get suspicious. One of the players may recognise some of my men, people in restaurants, in bars, in cinemas may be able to recognise them. So we turn to people from forces outside Florence – but we are still left with the business of motive, a reason for their presence that will not arouse suspicions. Turn them into sports journalists? Never. The players know the vast majority of Italian sports journalists.

'But with you, a foreigner, we have no such problem. Tozzi merely has to tell the boy that you are an English journalist writing a piece, or a series of pieces, on Continental football stars. You may even be writing for one of those American sports magazines. "In-depth" is the phrase a journalist would use, no? Tozzi adds that your object is to aim at realism, to attempt to get right inside the personalities involved. You've read some newspaper material on the two men, so you must know that Corrente will do whatever Tozzi asks him to do. It will work out smoothly, you'll see.'

'Except for the training,' I muttered.

'There's that,' Regalia grinned. 'But you're fit enough and young enough. Remember, you're an ex-Special Branch man, supposedly a professional at infiltration techniques.'

'And what will you be doing all this time?' I asked. 'Sitting on your backside out in the Borgo Ognisanti?'

Regalia's stare was bleak. 'Don't be ridiculous. Tozzi rang me yesterday morning at 10.17. Ever since then I've been buzzing like an angry hornet. Apart from yesterday evening towards eight o'clock.' His eyes began smiling.

I didn't think mine were. 'I didn't see you,' I said.

'You weren't looking for me, my friend. You were too busy trying to outwit Belmonte's chauffeur.'

'Ah,' I said. 'You were in the hotel?'

He nodded. 'I gave you a couple of minutes, then followed you out. Just to see how you operate, you understand.' He grinned quickly.

'Bastard,' I muttered. 'So, how many men are you detailing on to this case?'

He took pencil and notepad from inside his jacket pocket, scribbled, passed a slip of paper over. 'That's my home address and telephone number,' he said. 'Anything you want, you call.'

'Which doesn't answer the question, Regalia,' I said. 'How much cover do I have here?'

'Enough,' Regalia said.

'Listen, chum,' I grated. 'You think your men are there to protect *me*, you think again. Doesn't it occur to you that they may get in my way?'

Regalia's face paled. 'No, you listen. I don't try to tell you how to do your work, don't you try to tell me how to do mine. This is still a police case, Mann, don't forget that. I'm not stupid enough to indulge in room-searches and looking elsewhere for concealed weapons so that I can get something on you and then have to sit back and watch you smirk because you haven't yet got to your armament contact, or your place of concealment is too subtle for me to discover. But this is still a police matter, even if half the idea of hiring one of your breed came from Tozzi. Just get out there and do what you can.' He was staring past me.

'You're talking too much, Regalia,' I said. 'An innocuous question like that and already you begin to lather up.'

He murmured one word – second person, instructive, verb intransitive – expressive, advisory, not refined. And then he grasped my wrist very tight, pointed his chin up the road, kicked his chair back, threw some money on to the table-top and beckoned me to follow him.

6

A FEW YARDS down the road a tall, slim youth was walking across the front of a green Porsche. He was wearing a violet roll-neck sweater and tight-fitting trousers in light grey. His skin was olive-brown, the hair very black, his features regular. He was worth looking at, but never as appreciable as the girl standing by the passenger door.

She was also slim, medium in height with similarly delicate, pointed features. Her honey-blonde hair was long, elaborately styled, pulled up from her forehead, falling in long, soft waves about ridges of her shoulders. She was wearing enough eye make-up to repaint an aircraft-carrier. She laughed at something the boy said across the top of the car, throwing her head back slightly, revealing very white small teeth. Colourful blouse in yellow and crimson; black slacks, tight at thigh.

'That's your boy,' Regalia said. '*Il famoso* Gianni Corrente. We'll follow him.'

He led the way up the road, stopped opposite a wicked-looking Alfa Romeo 164 in dark blue.

'Christ God, Regalia,' I said. 'I thought Corrente was supposed to be under constant surveillance.'

'Relax, Mann,' Regalia growled as we climbed into his car. 'One of my men is tailing the boy.'

It was true. Corrente's Porsche took off up the road in a squeal of tyres and roar of engine. We waited until a grey Alfa Romeo without markings went after it, then cut into the traffic and joined the game.

'Who's that?' I said.

'Name's Mimmi. Youngish lieutenant. Good man.'

He was. He wasn't frightened to overtake Corrente as we all swept over the railway tracks that cut a vicious scar across the northern part of Florence.

The lunchtime traffic freeze had already begun to thaw out, making it easy enough to keep close watch on Corrente's car without having to approach too close.

The boy was driving steadily, occasionally turning his head to the right as he passed on some witticism to the girl in the passenger seat. Her head remained insistently turned in his direction.

We were approaching the Piazza San Marco by short turns. Mimmi's car disappeared from sight as we made a sharp right turn, then appeared again a few moments later from down a side-street. He gave no sign of recognition as we cut past his front fender, his dark, brooding face a perfect mask.

'He looks good, that Mimmi,' I said.

Regalia grunted. 'He damn well ought to,' he said. 'I trained the bastard.'

'Then again,' I said, and Regalia scowled.

Corrente eventually pulled up outside a small trattoria in a side-street just off the Piazza della Independenza. He was locking the door of the Porsche just as we went past, looking for a reasonable place to stop.

'You go in,' Regalia said.

'And you?'

He shook his head. 'Not me. I've other things to look after. But I thought it would be a good opportunity for you to have a look at the boy, try to catch the peculiarities of his conversation, get a picture of how his mind works. It'll all help.'

I got out of the Alfa, poked my head in before closing the door. 'And the girl?'

Regalia shrugged. He was staring straight ahead. 'We'll find out, perhaps.'

I slammed the door shut, watched him take off down the

54

street. A few yards past the door of the trattoria Mimmi was sitting in his car, doing the Regalia act of staring expressionlessly out of his windscreen.

I slipped along the pavement, looked in through the window, pointed towards the waistband of his trousers. 'Good stuff, Mimmi,' I said, 'but the gun's showing.'

His head came round, black eyes stared into mine, then his head swung back into the set position. Which all meant two things. First that Mimmi had been well brainwashed. Second, that Regalia hadn't been tardy in briefing some of his men as to the likely nature of my activities. If Mimmi hadn't been warned and informed as to my identity he would have been out of the car sharply, reaching for his metaphorical handcuffs.

I left his car and strode towards the doorway of the restaurant. I thought I might like Mimmi. The eyes and skin were darker, of course, but he reminded me of myself a few years earlier. Still an organisation man and with the fact stamped on to my features. Not unsympathetic, but as though any expression of personality was being forced to remain dormant and under tight control.

The restaurant was a badly-lit, quiet place that suggested an atmosphere of intimacy. A chubby waiter in white shirt, black trousers and thinning hair made his way towards me. Corrente and the girl were *in situ* at a table along the right-hand wall. In the far corner, with his back to them, was a character in a brown suit reading the daily paper and working hard at his teeth with a pick even though there were no empty, dirty plates nearby. I took him for a pre-prandial picker and chanced my luck. The place opposite his was vacant, backed by the wall.

Habits die hard, and the habit of being in corners, by walls, at the back of cinemas and theatres and restaurants, of always being behind any subject one is surveying or guarding – that habit dies very hard. You never see a fat man in a famine. And you never see someone killed from behind who doesn't look many times more piteous than

55

his cousin killed from the front. I settled into the vacant seat, ordered a drink, lighted a cigarette, listened and watched.

Corrente's voice was light, the accent very recognisably Sardinian, very much more pointed and guttural than the flat-tongued dialect of Central Tuscany. He and the girl chattered gaily of the cinema, of nightspots, of football, of fame, of love. They told each other slim jokes, exchanged light pleasantries, fought for each other's attention. Closer to they looked very similar in colouring and in the shape of facial bones like a pair that had wandered off the fashion pages of one of those trivial Italian weekly magazines. Everything about the rapport suggested the possibility that they had not known each other for a long time.

I ate a plateful of pasta, nibbled at some veal that tasted porcine, helped myself to some fruit, washed everything down with a modest half-bottle of Chianti and left as they were about to begin their last course. Neither of them appeared to evince any interest in my presence as I paid the bill and made my way out into the street.

The first bullet whined past my right ear, the second missed by several centimetres as I flung myself on to the pavement and made for the protection afforded by a red Fiat Panda parked almost directly outside the front entrance of the restaurant.

That's part of the trouble with trying to look casual. Time seemed to pass very slowly as I wrenched open my jacket and palmed the Beretta out of my waistband. God knows where he or she had been, but by the time I stuck my head out from behind the Panda's nearside front tyre, the pavement was as bare as the floor of a funeral parlour.

I rolled over on to my left side and saw the car taking off, an expensive Lancia Thema in pillar-box red swirling round the corner fifty metres away and out of sight.

I stood up, brushed off my clothes, tucked the gun away and allowed impressions to settle into my mind.

The first had been the thought of a silencer. But two bullets from a silencer. That made no sense. Silencers are fine for one-off work. After that they cause the damn gun to jam. All very quiet except for the sound made by your hand disintegrating into a nasty mess.

And the second thought had been Mimmi. Some well-trained cop that sat in his car and did nothing while some charming stranger tried to consign me to an early grave. Which made no sense at all, if he was really as good as Regalia had said he was.

* * *

I feared the worst the moment I looked in the direction of the grey Alfa Romeo. Mimmi was still behind the wheel, but the hard stare that had accompanied me into the restaurant was there no longer. The boy's body was flat against the back of the seat, but that bright-featured head had fallen forward.

I walked quickly towards the car, jerked open the door on the driver's side and felt the bile rise in my throat as all the familiar stenches attacked my senses. Urine, cordite, the rankness of death. Mimmi's left hand was still where it lay across his thigh.

I'd seen that posture before and I knew too well that his was the sleep of a man who would never again wake.

I undid the button of his jacket and it was there – a neat dark hole to the left of his chest, with just a splash of blood and those telltale grey powder stains around the periphery like iron filings drawn by magnetic force. I didn't have to remove his seat-belt or move his body to guess that the bullet had cut right into the leather seating behind him. No exit hole behind the seat.

The gun was still in the waistband of his trousers, slung to one side and over his right hip. A Beretta *calibre nove*. And the windows that had previously been open had now been rolled closed.

I rebuttoned the jacket, closed the door, spat sour saliva

on to the pavement and walked away as briskly as I could into the Piazza della Independenza nearby.

I made no attempt to wipe from the jacket-button or door-handle any finger- or palm-prints I may have bequeathed.

7

I CAUGHT A taxi at the end of the street, ignored the chattering of the driver and concentrated solely on the business of trying to get back to physical normality.

My mouth felt dry and bitter, and the cotton of my shirt was sticking to the skin at the small of my back and inside arms. It was not a particularly warm afternoon.

By the time I reached the hotel I felt marginally better, manifestly less disturbed. I took the lift up to the third floor, looked carefully at the door-handle and surrounds, couldn't see anything that suggested furtive intrusion on someone else's part.

Once inside the room I checked all my clothes, made sure all my markers were in place, paid special attention to the fire-resistant aluminium suitcase. It's a fancy affair with pig-skin trim and locks specially fitted by a backstreet expert in Vienna. No signs of tampering.

I peeled my clothes off, stood underneath the shower spigot for fifteen minutes, dried myself off and fell on to the bed.

* * *

Regalia's call came twenty-two minutes later.

'Mann?' he said, his voice flat and expressionless. 'Why not take a walk across the square?'

'I'll be with you in ten minutes,' I said.

'Make it five,' Regalia said, and put the phone down quickly.

I knew why he wanted me, and he knew why he wanted

me. But he was damned if he was about to let me know that he knew that I knew. Games, ploys, tricks; things – so many things – left unsaid.

* * *

The primary police arms in Italy are two. There is the *Polizia*, or the *Pubblica Sicurezza*, under the ministry for the interior and concerned with the business of maintaining public safety. And there is the *Carabiniere*, under the ministry for defence, rich in tradition; structured like an army; stable; undemonstrative; not unpopular with the citizenry, so many of whom have, or have had, relatives connected with the organisation. It is possible, though not common, for a young Italian to spend the period of his military service in the *Carabiniere*. The organisation is much larger in terms of manpower than its *PS* counterparts, and this, linked to its para-military structure and commonality, ensures for it a place in the hearts of the people. Gathering information – that is one of the *Carabiniere's* strengths.

All of which cannot disguise the fact that there exists a ridiculous duality of control between the two forces. Commit any crime and you have the choice to ring two alternative numbers. Both the *Pubblica Sicurezza* and the *Carabiniere* have uniformed men; both have plainclothes branches; both have special squads to deal with murder, with drugs, with kidnap, with rape, with theft; both have their squads of mobilised officers.

A confused and confusing situation. It is certain that the people concerned are well aware of the fact; equally certain that a welding-together of the two units would be impossible. Too many rivalries have been built up and prolonged, too many jealousies exist. The duality continues.

The headquarters for the Central Tuscan branch of the *Carabiniere* is in the Borgo Ognisanti, immediately next door to the church of the same name.

It is a strange edifice to look at, windowless at ground

level, with buildings leading to left and right of the central, square-doored entrance.

Just to the right of the doorway a marble plaque is built on to the wall, comprehensive in its detail:

CARABINIERI
COMMANDO GRUPPO DI FIRENZE
COMMANDO COMPAGNIA DI FIRENZE
NUCLEO INVESTIGATIVO
NUCLEO RADIO MOBILE DI PRONTO
INTERVENTO
STAZIONE FIRENZE PRINCIPALE
NUCLEO DI POLIZIA GIUDIARIA

I couldn't think of anything they'd omitted to mention.

Two middle-aged *carabinieri* in blue uniforms sat at the desked area just by the main doors trying not to look excessively bored. I asked for Regalia and they took one look at the English suit I was wearing and began to make a great fuss of me.

I walked along behind one of them, taking in the brown doors with their little plaques; the various doorways across the cloister; the dampness and chilliness of white-painted stone.

At the end of the colonnade we turned right, marched up stairs that broke to the left, crossed in front of more brown doors, passed open windows that gave onto the church across the other side of a cloister, finally stopped in front of a door with Regalia's name on it and the words – in capital letters – NUCLEO INVESTIGATIVO.

It was a large square office spatially divided into two sections. By the door was the 'relaxation area': a television set off in one corner, low-slung leather chairs grouped about a squat coffee table that bore magazines and newspapers.

The other section was strictly for business. A heavy-weight desk littered with papers, Regalia's backside firmly planted in a wooden armchair, two more flat-backed wooden chairs without armrests, some filing cabinets, two tables laden with files and papers.

The walls served to emphasise the intangible barrier. Above the leather chairs hung a pair of daintily-framed prints of medieval Florence. Behind Regalia hung a series of portraits which depicted stiff-backed *carabiniere* generals of the past, mustachioed, spurred, businesslike, self-conscious.

As I was shown into Regalia's office a tall, hollow-cheeked young man slipped out of the way, closed the door behind him.

Regalia didn't stand up to me. His dark eyes looked a little sad and mad at one and the same time.

'Those boys on the gate jumped when they saw me,' I said. 'Well-briefed. So who was that?'

'Lieutenant by the name of Baudini,' Regalia said. 'A good man.'

'As good as Mimmi was, or not?' I asked quietly.

Regalia flushed. 'Go to hell,' he said savagely. 'You've left the world of friendships and trust and mutual respect and admiration. You're dried up inside – ' He broke off, stared at me dully.

He knew from experience that excessive emotion often induces a compulsive tendency towards the use of clichés. As to his assessment of my emotions, maybe he was right, maybe not. To me it didn't have to matter; but I thought I could identify with the emotions he was experiencing.

'They're things about you we know, Mann,' he said.

I felt a cold finger crawling through the upper vertebrae of my spine. It went away, warmed off, at his next words.

'For instance, it was nice of you to leave those prints behind,' he said. He was staring at me intently.

I shrugged. 'It was a professional job,' I said, 'and that meant that the odds were heavily against our man not wearing gloves. But I couldn't take the chance of wiping off my prints and thereby eradicating any others that were there. I assumed you would have the sense to surmise that it wasn't me behind the gun.'

He laughed angrily. 'God knows, professional's the right word.'

'And you're thinking what I'm thinking?' I said.

'You're thinking what?' Regalia growled.

'I'm thinking that the number of men who have the nerve to kill in that icy fashion, that number is not so large. This was someone who was good enough to ignore all the rules. First, he fired just the once, he didn't have to place a second insurance shot, and to do that you have to be confident. Second, he rejected the notion of trying to keep some distance between his gun and the target. Third,' I paused, 'it appears that he is left-handed: for a right-handed man the angle round toward's Mimmi's heart would have been too sharp. He'd have had to damn nearly break his wrist.'

'And fourth,' Regalia continued, 'that boy Mimmi was no fool.'

'Exactly,' I said. 'So unless you think he was killed by someone who knew him well enough to dull his suspicions, my diagnosis stands. A professional, a crack man. And how many of the breed are there, Regalia? You tell me.'

He stared at me bleakly.

'You may be right about the question of whether the gunman was left-handed or not. He didn't puncture the oesophagus and that lies right behind the heart towards the centre.' He sounded as though he was talking for the sake of it.

'And the timing?' I asked.

'That's where you come in,' he said.

'Just as a check, I thought I came into Tozzi's office at the football club at two minutes after midday.'

'I made it five minutes after,' he said.

'So do your sums, Regalia. I looked at my watch as I walked into the restaurant and it read seven minutes short of two o'clock. I came out at 2.33. And Mimmi didn't look long dead when I saw him then.'

'Two fifteen to two twenty, then?'

I nodded. 'And the gun?'

'Browning .22 target pistol, hard-jacketed shells, probably a short barrel, possibly a fancy grip,' Regalia said.

'It's the sort of gun one of the boys would use for a job like that,' I said. 'And he may have had a silencer attachment. I've got an ear for the sound of pistol shots and I didn't hear a damn thing.' I paused. 'So why, Regalia? Who knew Mimmi well enough, who knew what he was up to?'

He didn't answer my question immediately. 'The Catholic Pole, Korensky, was last seen in Zurich. Dorpmanns in Amsterdam. Darouche and Mueller were making easy money by looking after some famous actors at a private blue-film festival in Frankfurt. It seems that several big stars have been shooting pornographic shorts with private directors. So they get together every now and then to compare ideas.' He looked as though he was about to spit in disgust. But the carpet was medium-pile, fancy-patterned, too good to play the role of spittoon.

'And Crawford?' I asked. 'Benkaddour. What of them?'

Regalia shook his head. 'No trace.'

'That's just marvellous,' I said bitterly. 'Crawford's no-one's idea of the perfect babysitter but alongside that little Arab bastard he behaves as sweetly as a girl on her first date.'

'You sound *too* bitter, my friend,' Regalia said. 'I thought we agreed that this killing was done by a left-handed merchant. My files tell me that both Crawford and Benkaddour are right-handed, but they've already been located in Frankfurt.'

He was either ingenuous, or trying to pull the wool over my eyes. I let it ride for the time being.

'So maybe there's a new man,' I said. 'Someone not on

your files. In a sense it doesn't matter. You still haven't given me the motivation.'

'The motivation,' he laughed bitterly, stood up, began to walk around. That meant *I* had to stand up, just to ensure that he didn't manage to get behind me. He saw me, worked it out, laughed again, this time more humorously. 'You never stop, do you?' He sat down.

I relaxed again, and followed suit. 'Never,' I said. 'The motivation.'

'And the motivation, God knows.' He began to talk quickly. 'I can't work out anything that makes sense from all angles. A private affair? Maybe, maybe not. That doesn't really fit. I mean, why should Mimmi find himself up against one of these characters? There's nothing known to this office that suggests strange extra-mural activity and I have these men checked out pretty thoroughly. Nice boy, good background, no political angles, no woman trouble. But if these Sardinians – and we can't ever pinpoint them – are hiring this sort of help it means many things: not least of which the fact that they must have some good money readily available to them. You people charge high enough rates. Just think what these other characters charge.'

He wasn't going to tell me anything that might be of help, so I made my way towards the door. When I reached it, I turned.

'Mimmi had a radio in his car,' I said. 'He didn't manage to get to it before he died?'

Regalia shook his head. 'No sign.'

I nodded at him. 'You know where to find me,' I said.

'And don't you forget it,' he growled. He wiped a hand over his weary face.

I slipped out through the doorway, closed the door behind me as gently as a philatelist cataloguing a rare stamp and made my way downstairs.

Coming up the stairs was a young *carabiniere* wearing stiff uniform and looking mightily pleased with himself.

I wiped the smile off his face by asking the way to the

switchboard area. He looked uncertain of himself for a moment, until I mentioned Regalia's name, and then his hands became very busy with directions. I thanked him and followed them.

Two girls were inside the telephone room. One was young and reading a magazine; the other was older and looking busy, her fingers flitting with activity like those of an addict at cat's cradles.

I leaned over the young one, gave her a big smile, roughened the English accent so that she automatically smiled at the comicality of its pronunciation and asked whether Mimmi had managed to ring through to headquarters before he'd been killed. The news didn't surprise or shock her.

She flipped an exercise book from the top of the switchboard, looked through it and shook her head, no. A light flashed in the board and she turned away. I picked the book up and peeked inside.

Looking through the notes for the previous day was intriguing. The book gave the extension numbers, the names that went with them, the date, the number required and the volume of units consumed.

Regalia was there in strength. As far as I could see he had dominated proceedings throughout that morning. A short call to London, then calls to Amsterdam, Paris, Zurich and Rome. The first four calls had lasted only a matter of a few minutes. The call to Rome had been placed at 10.47 and terminated at 11.09. And there had been a further call to London, one that had been placed at 11.13 and had lasted for nearly three-quarters of an hour.

The girl turned back to me, her temporary work finished. '*Dunque, niente da Mimmi,*' I said, and she shrugged.

I thanked her, returned the book, made my way out into the courtyard and passed the characters at the gate. They didn't snap to attention as I slid out into the street. Just those flat, cop eyes watching me as though I was something that badly needed to be knocked into a nice, squashy shape.

66

At that moment I didn't feel absolutely confident that they weren't right. There would have been bullet scars on the pavement and walls close to that restaurant. Regalia must have known about them, must have put two and two together. I didn't like the fact that he'd omitted to mention them. My life wasn't *that* cheap.

8

WAITING FOR ME back at the hotel was a bulky parcel, brown paper wrapped round files that contained what ever material Tozzi felt he could show me on the running of the Fiorentina football club.

With the parcel was a medium-sized man, in his forties, with watchful eyes, a jaw you could have hung hoops on, and wearing a charcoal-grey suit that suggested uniform.

He introduced himself as Giorgio Spezia, my intended chauffeur. He held himself well, his whole stance suggesting patient ability. I liked the fact that he was not too young, the expectation that he had solid experience on his side.

'And the car?' I asked.

He recited the facts off in a singsong baritone. 'Fiat Croma 2-0 CHT. Five forward gears, the top gear for use on long flat straights such as *autostrade*. Top speed 210–220 kph. Specially fitted radio that permits short-range transmission to our offices. Michelin steel-braced radials at high pressure.'

I stopped him. 'All right. So how much has Signor Tozzi told you about the contract?'

'Nothing, signor.' He stared impassively at me. 'Just that I am to take my orders only from you, from no-one else. That the hours might be long.'

'Good,' I said. 'Be here at seven tomorrow morning. Wait outside for me. We'll see then what the two of you can do.'

He nodded, was turning away to leave the hotel, when I

bumped into him. It was there on his left side, too obviously
a bad match between holster and gun.

Spezia jerked back, his eyes looking bitter.

'Was that Tozzi's idea?' I asked.

He shook his head unhappily. 'Mine.'

'It might not have been a bad idea once,' I said. 'But
either you've been reading too many thrillers or you haven't
worked in this league for some years. Times have changed,
Spezia. The heavy style is out, my friend. Now we think
our way through these affairs, we don't stand still, fire from
the hip, and hope for the best. We try to make sure of the
best. And that means being smart. Leave the gun at home.
I want a good driver, not a trigger-happy cowboy.
Tomorrow we'll see whether you drive well.'

I watched him walk away, still unhappy, his pride
obviously shattered.

* * *

With my check-off of the room completed, unable to
discover any signs of intrusion, I rang down to reception
for a glass of milk and some sandwiches, waited for them to
arrive, then settled down to Tozzi's material.

It wasn't easy. I was a long way from the beaten track.
This was no basic information on unlikeable characters, no
thorough breakdown of the physical characteristics of a
hotel or restaurant, no essential specification of a political
nature.

It was six hours later, close to midnight by the time I felt
I knew the material well enough to make use of it.

Training methods; information as to the age, height,
weight, history, talent, potential, achievement of each
player; a close look at the backstage organisation of Fiorentina. And there was the complicated data – the involvement of local businessmen in the financial running of the
place. Several of the directors were local agents for the
more prestigious Italian firms such as Pirelli, Olivetti, Fiat,
Alfa Romeo. One or two, Belmonte among them, were

entrepreneurs in their own right. One, Ario Pescaglini, was a wealthy exporter of Florentine leather goods. Another, Annabella Leone, was as extremely prosperous lawyer. Belmonte's money came from a thriving construction business. It was a lot of money.

Tozzi had been thorough. But he had also been self-effacing. He had sent me detailed information concerning the personalities and policies of all the staff of AC Fiorentina. All, that is, except the details relevant to his own *curriculum vitae* and present status.

A shy man, perhaps, this Tozzi.

*   *   *

Six fifty-nine the following morning found me nursing my third cup of breakfast coffee and staring out of the window of my room on to the damp square below. Midnight rain had fallen, freshening the air and light. Spezia was at station inside his car, a black Croma with sleek looks. I kept with him as he waited for his watch to move round to the prearranged time for the rendezvous.

Five minutes later he was still there, waiting for me. I liked that, the fact that he hadn't looked at his watch during that time. I liked also the fact that he hadn't come into the hotel. Both suggested that he might genuinely be cool and under control, able to take orders without questioning them.

I set the usual knick-knacks that would tell me whether anyone had searched my room in my absence, locked the door, hung the 'Do Not Disturb' notice on the door-knob and set off down in the lift.

The lobby downstairs was quiet, the only noises coming from the kitchen.

The car was parked in the vicinity of an early twentieth-century piece of statuary that I had noticed on arrival at the hotel. It depicted a muscular character wearing no clothes and having a wrestling-match with a lion. He was trying his damnedest to garotte the thing. The lion had its

71

mouth wide open and showed a nice spread of teeth. A fierce snarl, that meant business, that suited my current mood. If it was merely yawning I wasn't interested.

Spezia didn't move when he saw me come out into the square, didn't lean over to open the passenger door, didn't start the car.

I climbed in, sat down and looked around. It looked a comfortable car, not so low that it induced immediate claustrophobia, not so high that you might wonder about its ability to take tight corners without sliding.

Just one thing bothered me about Spezia. His white gloves. They looked an expensive item in soft leather, but the sight of them irritated me.

'Take them off, Spezia,' I said. 'The gloves.' He looked at me in surprise, then slipped them off, tucked them away in the cupboard in the dashboard.

'Never, never wear anything white,' I said. 'Shirt, tie, hat, gloves, shoes, suit. All neutral colours, wear those. I don't like white.' He was staring at me impassively, so I told him. I told him about men I had seen killed against a white background. I told him about men I had seen shot because at night the white of their shirtfronts had presented a simple target to trigger-happy gunmen.

'However much they're paying you, Spezia,' I said, 'I'll double. In return you do exactly as I tell you at all times. Don't ever stop to question any decisions I might make. All right?'

He nodded.

'First,' I said, 'first we'll go out on to the outskirts of the city to the east and have a look at the car. Then we'll strike north-east up towards Fiesole and have a look at you.'

He nodded, started the motor, pulled out smoothly into the square and placed us quickly on to the eastbound northern bank of the Arno.

Ten minutes of his driving and I was ninety per cent certain that both car and driver were what I was looking for. Spezia liked his gearbox, used the lower four gears incessantly, slipping smoothly from one to the other. He also knew his traffic-lights, could pace us between each without recourse to vigorous braking.

Once we were out of the city's environs he really put the Croma through its paces, taking the car up and down through the gearbox, showing me maximum and minimum speeds for each gear-change. We did some braking practice, enough to demonstrate that the car stayed true in line, never pulling to right and left. We found a stretch of tight corners, ran the stretch several times back and forth and the car held the road beautifully. On each turn we passed a postman delivering early morning letters. He thought we were mad. But Spezia took no notice of him, and that was the important point.

By the time we had finished it was nearly eight o'clock, perfect timing for what I had in mind.

I brought Spezia to a halt by the side of the road. 'What do you think of it?' I asked.

He shrugged. 'It's a good car,' he said.

'You've driven this model a lot?'

He shook his head, a short wave from left to right to left. 'Not a lot. Enough.'

I waited for him to continue, and waited in vain. Not the loquacious type, our friend Spezia.

'All right,' I said. 'So much for the car. Now for you. Get me to Fiesole. Go by the south bank of the river, cross at the Ponte della Vittoria, cross through the underpass to the north of the station, move up to the Piazza della Liberta, then you're on your own navigation. I want to be in that main square in Fiesole in minus ten minutes. And remember,' I added, 'you don't get caught by the *vigili urbani*.'

I had seen good driving in thick traffic before, but never anything to compare to the expertise of this boy. Eight o'clock is strictly morning rush-hour time in Florence, but Spezia drove as though every car-owner for a hundred miles around had been ordered to keep his vehicle off the road.

He cut razor-thin slices through the most congested areas of traffic, judged the timing of every set of traffic-lights to perfection. Between the station and the Piazza della Liberta he found himself comprehensively blocked, and sat there without ever exhibiting one germ of frustration or annoyance.

Once on the road to Fiesole he let himself go, overtaking expertly without ever jettisoning a reasonable margin on the part of the other road-users. The traffic was against us, short-distance commuters coming into Florentine offices for the day.

Under instructions, Spezia drove through Fiesole and up into the hill ridges above. Go there in high summer and it is a place where wandering tourists become woefully lost, a maze of small roads, badly signposted, seldom marked on any but the most detailed of maps. It was perfect territory for what I had in mind. Incessant rain would have served the purpose best. But I'm not God, I can't manufacture the damn stuff to order. A damp-run test would have to do.

I started by asking his routine questions, then moved on to more difficult ones. Questions about tyre-pressures, techniques on dry roads, techniques on slippery roads; facts and figures about gear ratios, the brakes, steering column, chassis; opinion as to the more crazy things committed on Italian roads. I argued with him when he said that driving in Italy is a matter of nerve, when he suggested that the Italians were crazy and noisy, but not suicidal like the French. The best place in Italy for cars, I said, that was Venice. Spezia grinned, but he carried on talking sense. He knew his stuff, Spezia. He really knew it.

Once that part of the affair was through I ordered Spezia off the road. The trees there were close together, but not so close that a car couldn't weave its way slowly around the approximate lanes they formed. For twenty minutes I kept Spezia at that, just watching and admiring his manoeuvrability technique. The driving-wheel of the Croma whirled round like a Catherine cracker as he drove, the rear of the car slewing round to left and right against each turn.

I took him back to the road, ordered him along until we came to a stretch that was approximately straight and flat. He was travelling slowly now, waiting for the next command, so I leant down on the handle of the door and tumbled out on my side.

It didn't take long to register, say all of point one of a second. I had barely enough time to stand up and wipe off my suit before Spezia had turned his car round and brought it to a halt close to where I had fallen.

'That was just a trial, Spezia,' I said before he had time to ask any questions. I pointed down the stretch of road, a straight perhaps a hundred and fifty metres long, slightly undulating but not so fiercely that the roof of the car would not always be visible.

'Take the car back there to the point just where the road falls away down the hillside. Then drive at me, hard and fast.'

He looked perplexed.

'Just do as I say, Spezia,' I said. I patted him across the shoulders.

He nodded his head, climbed into the Croma, drove off.

I fell to one knee and pulled the Beretta out of the soft-leather holster attachment, sewn on to the inside level of the waistband of my trouser. I checked it over, looked anxiously at the gun. It is the .32 calibre with the short barrel, a useful piece of armament without ever trying to seem impressive. Three years ago a backstreet gun expert in Paris had fooled around with the standard grip, giving it slightly more adhesion and texture by laying a strip of soft chamois skin over the metal plates.

The gun hadn't been used for a fair time, but I always made a point of examining it once every three or four days, checking the balance, grip barrel, trigger-and-action. It seemed fine.

I waited until Spezia was thirty yards away before firing close above the roof of the car. Then I dived out of his path.

He brought the car round to a motorcycle stop, swinging the back of the car to the right until he was slewing broadside along the road.

His eyes were mad. They had every right to be mad. Only a fool likes the notion of being shot at.

I opened the door of the Croma on his side and ordered him out at gunpoint. For a moment I thought he was going to rush me, but his eyes gradually began to lose their anger.

'You made only one mistake, Spezia,' I said, as he climbed warily out.

He nodded. 'I turned the car the wrong way.'

'Right,' I said.

He walked away from me, scooped up a handful of dirt from the roadside and rubbed it on to the rear number-plate until it became nearly illegible. 'You needn't have bothered,' I said as he straightened up. 'The police are supposed to be on our side in all this.'

He spat on his hand, wiped it on some grass. 'That's what *they* say,' he said darkly.

I put the gun away out of sight, smacked him across the shoulders, nursed him back under the wheel, offered to buy him a coffee.

He looked pleased at that. I felt pleased because I'd found a rare character: a professional wheelman who had excellent reactions, obeyed orders, and always drove to his limitations.

Boys such as Spezia are hard to find.

We drove back into Florence.

9

BELMONTE'S VILLA was set back from the road that curves ponderously between the eastern part of Florence and the small village of Settignano. Houses gather tightly at the edges of the road. Journey time from the centre of Florence – *circa* twenty minutes. It would have been faster but for the tardiness of the local trolleybus, whose driver insisted on squatting his vehicle firmly in the middle of the road, and some workmen in stained vests who made a great business of waving their green and red lollipop sticks to let us file slowly past a hole in the road.

Just as we were about to turn into the gravel driveway leading to Belmonte's house, a red Fiat Uno churned dangerously past us, climbing off noisily in the direction of Settignano village. A worse driver than Spezia might have placed his car in a compromising situation, and run the risk of a minor accident.

The village was a white-washed, red-tiled affair with a lot of fancy metallic trim built into the brick-red shutters, some tricky carvings in wood round the edge of the verandah that housed the front door, and a sea of gravel out front where the driveway belled out into a bulb.

A bottle-green Fiat Tipo with the fast-backed look sat quietly to the left of the house without trying to suggest that it could ever be the number one family car.

Spezia pulled our Croma alongside it, I climbed out, and peeked a look at the smaller cousin. Florentine number-plates and a lot of dust on the outside. Some woollen rugs on the back seat inside. And within the area of the pile of rugs something – just a suggestion – that looked familiarly like a hand-gun. I tried the doors of the car. They were locked.

I didn't feel in the mood to break open one of the car's windows, so I tramped up the steps that led to the verandah, looking for a bell or a knocker. No bell. No knocker. Just a collection of brass tubes hung in various calibres and lengths from a brass ring set into the stonework round the door-frame.

I flicked at the tube nearest to me, then stood back as the contraption tinkled a shrill scale into the morning air.

'He's not at home,' a low voice said behind me. Never move quickly unless you have to. I turned slowly to its source.

She must have moved well. The gravel along the drive and at the perimeter of the house had been loose, not firm, noisy under the wheels of the car, and I hadn't heard her coming.

She was medium in height and build, with strongly-muscled, narrow-ankled legs, an attractive woman trying hard not to betray the inevitability of cell degeneration. There was a shade too much flesh above the triceps and at waist and hip, but the face was handsome and well-boned.

She was wearing a beautifully-tailored dress in a royal blue that almost matched the colour of her eyes. Her hair was pale yellow, but it looked the sort of hair that would have been honey-blonde away from the bleach-bottle. Her mouth was wide-lipped and very red, a brilliant vermilion that matched her painted nails. White shoes, expensive stockings, fancy jewellery at wrist, neck and ear-lobe.

She was drinking – a pale amber liquid in sufficient quantity to float two ice-cubes off the bottom of a chunky tumbler.

'I'm Linda Belmonte,' the lady said. 'What do you want?'

'It's a bit early for that kind of thing, isn't it?' I said. It wasn't yet 10.15.

78

'It's my Scotch,' she said aggressively.

'Yours,' I said, 'or his. It doesn't matter. Is your husband here?'

She began to climb the steps towards me, stopped, jerked a hand upwards. 'Where he often is,' she said nastily. 'God knows he isn't here.'

'And wasn't here last night, either,' I said gently.

Her eyes were angry. 'Who says?'

'I say,' I said. 'There was rain here last night, not a lot perhaps but enough to wash down the dust between the gravel chippings along the length of the driveway. No evidence there of anyone or anything having passed out this morning. So either you're lying about your husband's whereabouts, or he travels everywhere by helicopter . . .' I left the sentence unfinished.

She stared sullenly at my face, then walked past me and the once-tinkling tubes, opened the front door and turned round. 'You'd better come in, Mr Mann,' she said.

I took my backside away from the rail of the verandah, followed her in, and found myself in a book-lined hallway with not a legible book in sight. All leather-bound stuff that looked as though it had been bought by the kilometre and transported by container lorry.

A white-painted staircase pulled away from the left-hand wall and spiralled elegantly out of sight behind an over-glassed chandelier. I followed the lady Belmonte into her reception room.

More bogus books, a lot of chic furniture, some undistinguished landscapes in water-colour, and the door to the drinks cabinet wide open.

La Belmonte was soon over there, freshening her drink from a bottle of Black Label. 'For being rude,' she said, turning, 'no drink for you.'

'That suits me fine,' I said. 'So how did you know my name?'

Her eyes widened. 'Why, Belmonte told me all about you, how strong you are, and so clever. You didn't think it

79

was going to be kept secret, surely, all this business. Who's the little man in the Croma?' Her eyes were mean again now.

'Damn Belmonte,' I said. 'He should have kept his mouth closed. Never mind the man outside.'

She flared up. 'Who the hell are you to tell my husband what he can and cannot say? *Macche stronzo Inglese*. You cheap life-taker.'

I made the old speech again. 'Wrong, signora,' I said. 'Saver, not taker. And to answer one question with another, why don't you keep your man at home instead of letting him run around Florence with whichever filly happens to catch his eye at whatever moment? Who is she, this one?'

She was controlling herself well, but there was no misinterpreting the bleakness that washed across her eyes. She took a gulp from the tumbler of whisky, then sat down in a cream-leather chair with arm-rests the size of airstrips, in a manner that showed a lot of leg.

'I wish I knew, and I'm glad I don't know,' she said. Her eyes suddenly became cunning. She pointed a long exquisitely-nailed forefinger in my direction. 'Why don't you find out for me? You're clever, Belmonte says, you find out.'

I shook my head.

'I'll pay well,' she said. The idea was growing ever more attractive to her, nastier to me. 'Belmonte may be an unfaithful bastard, but he never keeps me short as far as money is concerned.'

'Nothing doing,' I said. 'Sneaking around failed marriages, that's not my line of work.'

'But if you happen to come across anything, you'll tell me?' she was trying to simper now. It didn't suit her.

'Maybe,' I said. 'And maybe not. You know damn well I may have to find out something about Belmonte's night-life, check up on this girl of his, ascertain whether or not he has told her anything about this business concerning Corrente. You know all that. So stop playing coy.'

She stood up, glared at me again, moved for the drinks cabinet once more.

'That's another thing,' I said. 'This drinking. How long has Belmonte been fooling around on the side?'

She stared hard-eyed at me over the top of the whisky bottle.

'*Stronzo*,' she muttered.

'There are private detectives,' I continued. 'Don't pretend you haven't thought of them or used them before. Why not this time?'

She kicked the door of the drinks cabinet closed. 'Nosy bastard, aren't you?' she said. Her face was paler than it had been moments earlier.

'Sometimes I have to be,' I replied. 'Sometimes people's cupboards are full of skeletons. I like to watch them come tumbling out.'

'Yes?' Her eyes weren't hard any longer, just worried deep inside. 'Well, I did have him followed once. He found out, then threatened to have me thrown out.' She flopped down into a chair.

'And you don't leave,' I said, waving my hand around. 'Because of this?'

'Why not?' she said defiantly. 'He looks after me well. Why not?'

'Because there's dignity and dignity,' I said. 'One is the real article, founded firmly on self-respect, on the knowledge that you are at peace with yourself. And the other? That's just based on false premises, on material satisfaction. Take your choice.'

She shrugged.

'Why, for instance,' I went on, 'why did you marry Belmonte when you did, and not two years earlier when you gave birth to his child?'

That took her apart. The lower half of her face fell, the upper half became creased.

'Look, signora,' I said. 'This is part of my business, digging into the background of each case before I set to

81

work. Two nights ago Belmonte might have classified me as a bodyguard and you might have conjured up a neat portrait of some hairy-chested simian who was all muscle and no thinking matter. Don't make the mistake again, and don't stay with that mistake this time. Sometimes, as in this business, someone gives me a spade and shows me which part of the ground I should be turning over. Other times, it isn't made easy for me. But on all occasions I make damn sure that the whole garden gets turned over, not just the part that I've been recommended to cover. And that's how I come across these occasional snakes' nests of duplicities and tangental idiocies. So tell me about your daughter now, and save yourself some heartache later on.'

Her face was ashen now, and alcohol had nothing to do with its pallidity.

'You're just guessing,' she hissed.

'Some,' I said, 'not all. I know about the daughter. What I don't know is her present whereabouts, the name she travels under. I'm guessing about Belmonte.'

'Your guess is wrong,' she said. She stood up, her drink still half-finished. 'You'd better leave now.'

'Look,' I said. 'If you've anything to tell me, tell me now. The chances are high that I'll find out eventually.'

She shook her head. 'No,' she said. 'Leave now. Please.'

I stood up. 'You're making a mistake, signora. I know you know that and my knowledge of your knowledge upsets me. I'll dig it up. And you may get hurt. And don't start getting bitter about it all then, when it's too late.' I paused. 'You'll know where I'm staying if you want to contact me?'

She didn't reply, so I walked to the door, out through the hallway, on to the verandah, down the steps, across the gravel and stepped into the car.

Spezia took us gently along the driveway and on to the road for Florence.

Parked a hundred yards down the hill was a red Lancia Thema. Behind the controls was a thin-faced man wearing dark glasses with a gilded frame and reflecting lenses. A self-conscious toughman. He made the mistake of trying to tail us.

Spezia lost him within two minutes. But not before I made a note of the car number. I sensed that we'd see him again.

10

SPEZIA TOOK ME to the Viale dei Mille and this time there was no nonsense.

I had hardly closed the door to the reception area behind me before the commissionaire was out of his seat, making obsequious noises, and guiding me tenderly towards Tozzi's office.

'Signor Tozzi has not yet arrived, signor,' he said. 'He told me to tell you he would be here at eleven.'

It was ten minutes short of that time. I nodded. 'I'll wait,' I said.

'Si, signor. You wish something to drink?'

'Un caffelatte,' I said. 'Un po' di zucchero.'

'Si, signor. Subito.'

He was back with a large bowl of coffee in double-quick time, smiled at me, nodded, bowed, let himself out of the room. God knows what propaganda Tozzi had spread abroad on my behalf, but that commissionaire had metamorphosed into one very servile character since I had last seen him.

I poked around in the bookcase to one side of Tozzi's desk. It was full of newspaper clippings, instruction manuals and books, some novels, a series of annual textbooks on Italian football entitled *Almanacco Illustrato del Calcio Italiano*.

I picked out a well-used edition that gave all the information and statistics regarding the previous season – and there he was, after searching for a couple of minutes.

He had played that season for the Genoese team, Sampdoria, but his full biographical note was contained at the start of the book. **TOZZI Dino – Mediano e mezz'ala; altezza m. 1.80, peso kg 75; celibe** – had been born in Signa, just to the west of Florence, then acquired and developed as a midfield player by Modena, and had moved on to play for two seasons with Bologna and one with Fiorentina before being transferred to Sampdoria.

Not a particularly distinguished career. No really prestigious clubs in that list; no Juventus, no Inter, no Milan, no Napoli, no Roma, no Torino. He had spent several seasons with Sampdoria, but there was no evidence towards the end of the book that Tozzi had been blessed with the accolade of a career in the Italian national side.

I looked in a copy of the *Almanacco* for several years later. Tozzi had moved on to be coach of Squadra 'Primavera' of Fiorentina, the youth team, but he had retired as a player without ever having the immense pride and satisfaction of having been selected to play for Italy. I put the volume back, moved away from the bookcase. And that was when he came in through the door, looking slightly flustered and out of breath.

'I'm early,' I said. 'The commissionaire looked after me well. You don't mind?'

'Of course not,' he replied. His eyes were flicking round the room, disturbed and disturbing.

While he was taking off his coat, I wandered over and looked out along what length I could see of the boulevard outside. Parked fifty yards down the road to the left and only whispering distance away from Spezia and his car was a red Lancia Thema. Inside it was a man wearing dark glasses with reflecting lenses.

I turned from the window. 'I'm in your hands,' I said. 'I read all the material you sent me last night. It was fine, very useful. The only gap I can think of concerns you.'

He nodded. He didn't seem surprised, but I couldn't yet tell whether he thought he was bluffing.

'So why don't you tell me now?' I said. 'If you think you have time.'

'Plenty of time,' he said. 'I thought we might have a bite to eat at midday. Then I can take you along to the ground and show you around before the boys begin to turn up for training.' He paused. 'By the way, I rang Gianni Corrente a few moments ago and gave him a quick word of propaganda about you. Just the bare bones. You don't mind?'

I shrugged. 'That's fine,' I said. 'Now tell me about yourself.'

He nodded, walked about, settled himself behind his desk. I sat down in the easy chair Regalia had occupied twenty-three hours previously.

'There isn't much to tell,' Tozzi began. 'I was born virtually down the road, in Signa, was fairly bright as a boy. When I left school I spent some months at Rome University studying philosophy, then decided to abandon the ideal of a university education when the Modena club offered me professional terms. Perhaps it was a mistake. I don't know. Certainly I've had an interesting time in football, and I've never regretted the decision I made then.'

'And you stayed at Modena?' I asked.

He shook his head. 'I was transferred to Bologna, then made my way to the Genoese club, Sampdoria, where I stayed until I was no longer a first-rate player.' He was staring intently at me. 'Instead of moving to another club in a lower division, I stayed with Samp, as an *allenatore minore*, coach to the youth team. Then I came to Fiorentina. Not a particularly distinguished career, is it? No international caps, no great glories or fame.'

I smiled. 'You don't appear to have done too badly for yourself. In any case it often happens that the most talented practitioners of a subject often make the worst instructors. And vice-versa. This seems to be your *métier*, this business, the art of coaching.'

Tozzi looked at me intently. 'I think so,' he said slowly. It was as if he thought that my remark had been intended

87

as a slight, as though someone had at some time uttered disparaging thoughts about players and coaches, with the venom of their attack directed very much towards the latter, away from the former.

I took him up on that. 'Don't be so touchy, Tozzi. Doing these things involves first and foremost a physique that can adapt. Teaching them – now that is a very different matter. Me, by training I'm a teacher. Tell me,' I said, 'the book I looked in said you played as a *mediano, a mezz'ala*. Midfield player, you used to be, right?'

He paled. 'What book?'

I pointed towards the bookcase. 'One of those,' I said. 'You had just started your career with Modena. There was a barely recognisable picture of you on the opposite page. Very earnest expression, very short hair.' I grinned at him.

He grinned back vaguely. 'I was very shy in those days, completely unsure of myself, away from home for the first time.' He began to look as though my untruth had been accepted. 'Come on,' he went on, 'let me take you down the road to the ground and show you what facilities we have down there.'

He didn't wait to put his coat on, but the day was no warmer then than at the moment in which he had come into the room.

'By the way,' he said as we were leaving. 'I forgot to ask about your chauffeur. Is he good?'

I nodded. 'He's fine,' I said. 'And the car will do. There are faster cars and there are more malleable cars, but this one suits me very nicely.'

He didn't ask me any further questions. So it was invidious to point out that lousy cars can often be driven effectively by good wheelmen, that smooth machines can be useless in the hands of bumpkins. But then, I couldn't be positive that he was really uninterested.

11

THE MOMENT TOZZI and I stepped out of the hallway of the building and into the autumnal coolness of the street I sensed that something was wrong. Just one piece missing from the jigsaw that my mind had projected.

I looked quickly around until I had found the source of my temporary irritation. And as in all circumstances such as this, once I had found it the thing seemed as plain, as obvious as the clothes one stood up in.

The red Lancia Thema was still parked in the space where I had last observed it, from the window of Tozzi's office. But the would-be hoodlum in the reflecting dark glasses was missing.

I flicked my eyes down the street in the direction of the bar at which Regalia and I had been twenty-four hours earlier. A head of black hair atop reflecting lenses ducked out of sight behind the privet hedging that bordered the area *al fresco*.

We strolled casually towards the bar, firmly on our way towards the stadium. Tozzi was hanging to the left, close to the wall. I was outside, street-side of him.

I took a stab in the dark.

'That crazy boy in the red Lancia and the *dolce vita* sunglasses,' I said. 'Who is he, Tozzi?'

I hadn't turned towards him but from the corner of my eye could see his face swivel round in my direction.

'I don't know,' he said quickly.

Then, then I looked towards him. I slowed to a halt. 'Not good, Tozzi,' I said. 'You didn't sound inquisitive enough. Not inquisitive enough at all. "What man?" "Which Lancia?" Those are the kind of questions I was expecting to be – and should have been – asked.' I stopped, looked at him intently. The skin, the lines of his face had fallen into a mash of misery, the eyes were damp and terribly uncertain. I grinned at him quickly. 'Well, it appears you're not about to tell me. So I'll just have to find out on my own account, won't I?'

I moved off quickly down the street, could hear Tozzi following me, came level with the bar and looked in over the greenery into the tabled area within.

Two elderly gentlemen were drinking *grappa* and making a professional job of not communicating with each other. In the other corner, towards the asphalt of the road, was my man – light-grey slacks, tenderly-polished shoes in soft black leather, and a copy of the Florentine daily newspaper, *La Nazione*, curtaining off the top half of his body.

I waited at the edge of the genuine pavement for Tozzi to catch up and for our friend to lower his paper. The former was breathlessly prompt. The latter was not.

Notwithstanding this fact, patience was not the man's *forte*. Tozzi and I had stood *à deux* for only a few seconds before one corner of the newspaper was slowly curled down and the magnified fly-eye of one sunglass lens came into view.

Closer to he looked older than his style in hair and clothing might have suggested. He looked my age, and that's not young. Not old. But neither of us would have qualified to figure prominently in any Adonis competition.

I smiled pleasantly at him. 'We haven't met,' I said cautiously. 'The name is Mann. But then you might already have ascertained that fact from having followed me around all morning.' I dropped the lower part of my face back into the set position. 'Now, why don't you just go ahead and tell me who *you* are and what your particular game might be.'

He just continued to stare at me, so I leant over until my

face was only inches away from his. A nice aftershave lotion he was wearing. I told him so. Then I reached up and tweaked off the fancy dark glasses.

He didn't move. Perhaps his nostrils flared, perhaps a nerve in one cheek gave a momentary shudder. That was all. And it was easy to appreciate the why and the wherefore.

One of the eyes was fine. It was dark brown, damp, alive. The other was none of these things. The colour had been matched, of course, not perfectly, but it was a glassily dead thing, staring ahead like a fixed beam.

The good eye glared at me savagely. I couldn't afford to pussy-foot the issue.

'A one-eyed investigator,' I said harshly. 'That's an opening for a sick private-eye joke.' I turned to Tozzi. 'You really pick them, don't you?' I said.

He looked mystified, opened his mouth as if in reply, thought better of it, closed and pulled his lips into a tight line.

Suddenly I felt terribly unsure of myself, wanted to retreat, admit the fact that I might have made a psychological error, compensate for the feeling that I had gone too far too fast in the wrong direction. But the thing was decided for me by our new acquaintance.

Throughout the one-way converstion the upper part of his body had remained motionless, the lower part not. Those expensive shoes of his had been inching their way backwards across the cementing, sliding into a position that might platform a spring. And they finally reached the set position as my mind leapt to the right conclusion.

I swivelled to my left, sucked my stomach in, arched my back agonisingly as his right arm snaked out past the edge of the newspaper it had been holding.

In thrillers, knives and guns always 'gleam dully' when paraded in the open, irrespective of whether the locale for the appearance of the weapon in question is broad sunlight or gothic candlelight.

In real life it isn't like that at all. You worry about just one thing: whether the damn thing can do you any harm. And this particular specimen of a knife had precisely that in mind.

He was wiry, my friend, but still not properly set, his balances still awry. I clamped the fingers and thumb of my right hand around the man's wrist, pressing down; shot my left hand upwards around his upper arm and pulled hard in opposite directions against the elbow joint.

It all sounds childishly easy. In reality, not so. You have to be perfectly balanced, your arms have to be comprehensively free. But once you're close to making contact and have access to the right holds, it's an impossible one to resist. No-one prefers to wander around with wrenched muscles near the shoulder-joint and torn ligaments near the elbow.

His fingers agonisingly curled away and straightened; the knife fell noisily on to the cement flooring. But not one sound did he utter. His face was a frightening thing to look at, the perspiration along forehead and across bridge of nose out of character when set against the elegant casualness suggested by his clothing; the contrast between the livid hatred of the one eye, the pallid deadness of the other, never more marked.

I stamped on the knife, levered my one-eyed friend into his seat, released the hold I had on his arm, moved away a pace and sneaked a quick look in Tozzi's direction.

His eyebrows were up near his hairline in fright, his mouth was slightly open, he was breathing noisily, his face was also damp.

I looked quickly back to One-Eye. His left hand was kneading the muscles in the upper right arm. I knelt down and picked up the knife, ran a finger and thumb over its area. Technically it was a dagger rather than a knife, with both edges tapered and honed, the blade long in relation to the handle. An ugly beautiful weapon, a potential killer.

I still couldn't get the whole business into perspective; the fact that he had sat there immobile with the weapon hidden behind the newspaper. No sense. No rhyme or reason beyond the obvious ones.

I kept the dagger in my right hand, leant over, ran my left hand quickly across the front of his jacket, couldn't feel any bulge that suggested gun or wallet.

I leant back, tried to keep my voice low. It wasn't easy. 'Get out and stay away,' I murmured.

The absence of any wallet deprived me of a chance to get basic information, but grilling people in public places – that was not my line of country. I had the car number, which would lead me to whatever basic information I needed.

I picked up the dark glasses, returned them to him, ordered him up with a flick of the knife. 'And next time, my friend, no second-rate tricks. You'll have to come up with nothing, or something pretty damn good. You may not live so long in any case.'

For a moment I fancied that one edge of his upper lip lifted into a suggestion of a sneer. Then he slid away, tucking the fancy dark-glasses on to the bridge of his nose.

* * *

I watched him move away, then took Tozzi's arm.

'We're leaving,' I said.

He opened his mouth as if to ask a question.

I shook my head. 'Later,' I said. 'Let's just get out of here.'

I snatched a look at the two old men. They were staring blankly in our direction. Perhaps it had been the speed of the little scene that had failed to make any manifest impression. Or something else? Perhaps scenes such as that were a hundred a lira on Italian television and in the press. They probably thought we were character actors have a quick rehearsal for the benefit of a camera hidden in the privet border.

12

'GOD, I PLAYED that one all wrong, Tozzi,' I said as we moved away. He was walking close to my left side, and peered up inquisitively into my face.

'I looked at it from his point of view, not yours,' I explained. 'That was the mistake. I should have believed you, perhaps, but you hadn't been entirely honest with me and I chose the aggressive alternative. He knew you – that applies to both theories. But you could have been aware of him without knowing the extent of his knowledge about you.' I stopped, both talking and walking. 'You can see what I'm getting at?' I asked.

He hesitated for the fraction of a second, then nodded slightly.

'Why didn't you admit to the fact that you had seen him before, perhaps on several occasions?'

I began walking again; when he was abreast of me, continued.

'How long have you been aware that he was following you?' I asked.

'Yesterday afternoon.'

'When then? You must be precise.' I hadn't kept the impatience out of my voice. 'I'm sorry,' I said lamely. 'Just tell me when yesterday afternoon.'

'After training. Say four o'clock.'

'And again?'

'I wandered out on to the balcony of the sitting-room of my flat before turning in for sleep last night.'

'This morning?' I asked.

'When I arrived at the office just now,' he said.

'Of course,' I said. I shot a quick sidewise look in his direction. 'And you have no idea as to who he is or why he might be tailing you?'

He was staring ahead unhappily. 'I don't know him,' he murmured firmly. 'And the why. That I don't know either.'

I nodded. 'I'll find out, Tozzi,' I said. I laid a hand on the arm of his jacket. 'You leave it to me, just try to forget about it all.'

* * *

We stopped for an aperitif and a brioche at the bar almost opposite the AC Fiorentina stadium.

A handful of fans had already gathered to discuss team formations, training methods and the like. Surnames and jargonist phraseology hung in the air like stardust. Tozzi was stared at respectfully, the service from behind the bar was cheerful and prompt.

We moved away from the bar and into one corner. 'You seem popular enough,' I said, once we had settled down into plastic chairs round a plastic-topped table.

Tozzi was still pale, still unsure of himself. He had had a glimpse into a world foreign both to his nature and his unbringing and the experience must have nicked his psyche. Not a wide scar, certainly, but a quick touch with a sharp point, and in turn my remark had been very pointed, and – I hoped – astute. I wanted to get him back on to the sort of territory he knew really well. And it seemed that he wanted to retreat there of his own volition.

'For the time being,' he replied softly. 'But then, the team has played well recently.' He shrugged. 'You should see some of these people when we lose a match or two. Then they can often become extremely unfriendly.' He grinned. 'And that's the understatement of the year.'

I nodded. 'Fickle, maybe. But they appear to me to have a basic respect for you that transcends the vicissitudes of the game. Even in defeat they will look for excuses not to attack you personally. Or is that too simplified?'

'This isn't a wealthy club,' he replied. 'And the passions run higher in ratio to the amount of money involved. The big teams from the industrial cities of the north — that's where the ulcers come and go every other second.' He paused, grinned again quickly. 'Hell, I've been here so long they think I'm part of the local architecture.'

He was being modest. He was modest. But what I learned of his subject told me that it was rare to find any incumbent of a managerial chair staying *in situ* for more than a handful of seasons. Many are firmly on the merry-go-round of annual or biennial change between the various clubs. And it's all too easy to slip down the slope into managing a team of incompetents in the lower divisions.

My thoughts were interrupted a few moments later by the appearance in the bar of a hollow-eyed, hollow-cheeked, hollow-chested man, not tall but with finely-chiselled features and wearing a beige-coloured raincoat with the belt twisted into a knot across his belly. Beneath the hem of the raincoat the legs of the dark-blue trousers were rumpled, the black shoes scuffed and uncleaned; above the forehead the black hair was tousled and undisciplined. Only his eyes failed to communicate a general aura of casual shabbiness.

He eschewed the custom frequent to Italian bars of purchasing a clip from the girl behind the till, ordered a *caffe* at the bar, threw half a kilo of sugar on top of the coffee, swirled the cup vigorously and anti-clockwise for a few seconds. He then tipped the mixture down his throat, and some coins on to the bar. Not once had he stared in our direction, but within the space of a short moment he was standing by our table, one hand on Tozzi's right shoulder, the other firmly in the right pocket of his raincoat, both sharp brown eyes fixed on my face.

Tozzi gave a quick glance up, made a half-hearted attempt to rise from his chair, sank down again, shook hands with the newcomer.

'Angelo, *ciao*,' he said. He looked across in my direction. 'Harry,' he said. It was the first occasion on which he had been placed in the position of leader, the first time he had referred to me by my given name, and it sounded most obviously forced. 'Harry, this is Angelo Giacon, good friend and a fine football journalist. Angelo, Harry Mann.' He paused, looking unhappily at Giacon. 'Harry here is writing some articles for an English magazine about Gianni Corrente. Mostly human interest material. What sort of adulation the boy receives; how he trains; his private life, that kind of thing, you know.' His voice was pitched higher than I had yet heard it.

Giacon and I shook hands, looked at each other warily. I couldn't be absolutely sure as to the expression my face was wearing, but his was as suspicious as the face of a detective who had been lied to ten times a minute for ten thousand minutes.

'*Piacere*,' Giacon murmured. He continued to stare at me, but his next remark was firmly directed towards Tozzi. 'You're moving along to the stadium soon, Dino? Perhaps I can have a talk with Signor Mann while you're changing.' His eyes looked bleak, uncompromising.

I smiled, debonair, full of bonhomie. 'I'll look forward to that,' I lied.

Tozzi looked at his watch. 'That could be later, Angelo,' he said. 'Harry hasn't yet had the chance to meet, and talk with, Gianni. I want to introduce them personally. You'll understand?'

Giacon nodded abruptly. 'Of course.'

Tozzi kicked his chair back. 'But we can walk across together, no?' He was staring intently into my face, as though to convey the message that he didn't want to leave me alone with Giacon for longer than was absolutely necessary. It served to confirm my original impression by instinct Giacon was as trusting as a cobra.

Several journalists and sycophants were waiting in small groups to one side of the vast steel doors that led through into the north-west corner of the ground. They were prompt with their murmurs of '*Buon giorno*', '*Ciao*', '*Dino*', and with

98

their handshakes, as we cut through them. Giacon stayed behind to talk with them.

I was glad to be temporarily rid of him and voiced my sentiment to Tozzi.

He agreed with alacrity. 'You're so right about him. He's really an excellent reporter, writes well, knows the game inside-out from a tactical point of view. But is also a stupendously successful gatherer of information. Time after time I have read stories in his newspaper that were supposedly intended to be kept secret. He has numerous, and manifestly well-informed, contacts; he has energy in abundance; and most important, he is a subtle psychologist.' He paused. 'You know your job better than anyone else, but I'd like to give you a word of advice if I may.'

I nodded. 'Go ahead.'

'If I advised you not to pretend to be anything you're not, you'd have to laugh at me. But in Giacon's company, it would be best if you were to play the thing as straight as possible.' He mentioned a well-known British sports journalist to me. 'You know Brian?'

'I know of him,' I replied. 'They say he is the best-informed man in his line of country. Certainly he writes most of the others off the page in terms of style and intelligence.'

'Of course,' Tozzi said. 'He is very good. But Giacon knew him well when he was working as a journalist here in Italy.'

'I didn't know that,' I said.

He frowned. 'That's what I mean. There are bound to be many intricacies that are unknown to you, that you could only learn over a longish period of time. Be careful.' He shrugged. 'Come on, let's find some clothes for you to wear.'

I grabbed his arm just as he was about to duck through the doorway that led to the dressing-room.

'Let me just have a quick look at the stadium,' I said.

Tozzi looked at his watch, looked up, nodded. 'Quickly

99

then,' he said. He led the way up through a staircase of planks laid across a skeleton of scaffolding.

From the outside the stadium had suggested height, the lip of the terracing hanging high above concrete cantilevered pillars and overshadowing the forecourt near the entrances beneath. The impression of height had been accentuated by the four towering pylons that held the batteries of floodlights.

Within the elipsoid the impression given was not of height but of space, even of a flatness not hinted at by the exterior.

To the right of where we stood rose the main stand. The seating plush and not-too-plush; the curve of the directors' box down to the front; the press and television area tucked up aloft just underneath the edge of the huge overhanging concrete roof, comprehensively glassed in.

Round in a vast curve swept the terracing, stepped steeply, broken opposite the half-way line of the pitch by a tall, arrowed radio tower. And beyond was a romantic vista of bright-brown rooftops, of sepia-sloped, tree-topped hills stretching from north through east to south.

Ringing the pitch in a dirt-red oval strip was a cinder running-track; between that and the various enclosures for the spectators was an eight-foot high wire fence, the iron stanchions close together.

Empty of people, the place was ghostlike, eerie, unjustified, unreal. A place so obviously constructed as a meeting-place for humanity can seem only a bastard when that humanity is not present. And as a locale for bodyguard work the place was neither more nor less than a nightmare.

I ran my eye around the curve of the ground, turned back to Tozzi. He was standing close to my side and watching me intently.

'I've known all along that it would be near impossible,' I said. 'But just seeing it, having it placed in front of me like that, it's the hell of a thing. Only God could guarantee anything pacific in conditions like these.'

Tozzi's furrows were back where they belonged. 'You haven't seen the Meazza Stadium in Milan,' he said. 'That seems twice the size of this and the angle of the terracing is several degrees steeper.'

'I told you before, Tozzi,' I said. 'I can't promise anything.'

'I know,' he replied. 'But you'll try, won't you?'

I stared at him, into the stadium, into the sky, into the ground and waited for him to lead the way down below.

While his back was turned I transferred the Beretta out from the holster attachment sewn into the waistband of my trousers and into the right-hand pocket of my jacket. That was one little item that might trigger off dressing-room gossip that would be best left unthought and unsung.

13

FLESH EVERYWHERE. Light, dark, haired, hairless, scarred, dry, damp, oily.

For example, the first thing that caught my eyes as we entered the changing-rooms was the sight of a player being pummelled by one of the *massagiatori*. The boy was lying face-down on the massage-table, naked from the waist downwards, his eyes closed, his face damp with sweat, his white buttocks shivering in sympathy with the beating being administered to his thighs. The *massagiatore* was a thick-set man of middle age and height with little hair, the dead stub of a cigarette attached to one corner of his mouth, and large hands. They moved in vigorous latitudes and longitudes, kneading, slapping, stroking, rubbing, the smell of embrocation pungent in the air.

Tidy the place might have been minutes earlier, but now it was a market-place of track-suits, shirts, shorts, socks, boots. Laces and pieces of tape lay in piles on the floor like pale flattened worms.

Gianni Corrente was in one corner of the room, naked except for a brief pair of trunks. His torso was slim, tidily-muscled and hairless; his legs less hairless and strongly muscled. 'Heavy below the waist' would have been the clichéd phrase applied by a sensational magazine. Round his neck was a gold chain and crucifix, the latter squat and thick, badly proportioned. He was playing with the crucifix with his right hand, staring at the floor, unmoving and deeply retreated into harsh thought or light daydream.

He jerked his eyes up as the sounds of greeting by the

other players towards their manager reached his ears. For a moment the eyes tried to focus, return to reality; then they relaxed.

Tozzi put one foot up onto the bench on which Corrente was sitting, put one arm on to a shoulder.

'Gianni, *ciao*,' he said. He nodded in my direction. 'This is Harry Mann, the journalist I mentioned to you on the phone this morning.'

Corrente didn't attempt to get up, but gave a quick nod, a boyish smile. '*Piaccre*,' he said.

'Harry may have many questions for you, Gianni, and you'll see a lot of him in the next few days. For now we thought it might be useful for him to join our training sessions, see how we do these things at close quarters. Stay close to him and he'll probably have enough silly questions to keep your head buzzing. *Beh*, these journalists,' he finished. He grinned at Corrente, grinned at me; I grinned back and gave Corrente a quick smile. All very jolly. The Three Wise Monkeys.

'Clothes,' I said. 'If that isn't difficult for you.'

'Of course,' Tozzi replied. I didn't have to do conversions to give him the relevant information. Travelling fairly extensively on the Continent had made me adaptable: I was becoming an English prototype of Metrication Man.

'Shoes at size forty-two, that's the important thing,' I said.

'The other stuff can always be made to fit, no?'

Tozzi scurried off in search of one of the *massagiatori*. I watched him closely as he talked to one of their number at the far end of the room, then began to undress.

'You look fit,' Corrente said as I took my shirt off. 'At least, for a man who must spend much of his time sitting on his bottom behind an office desk.' He was staring at me cautiously.

I shrugged. 'It isn't bad,' I said noncommittally. 'Sometimes you have a chance to get exercise.'

Tozzi came back at that moment to save me further

embarrassment and with a bundle of clothing – track-suit in the Fiorentina colours of blue with purple trim, a pink fleur-de-lys badge on the upper part of the suit and to the left. There were a pair of socks, shorts, jersey, a new jockstrap, some lightweight boots.

I changed quickly in tandem with Tozzi. His body was still fairly trim, but there was a sag in the belly and I suspected that his legs would pinken badly if asked to undergo more than moderate exercise.

Many of the players had already left the changing-room by the time we were both ready. Corrente went over to one corner of the room, found a practice-ball, flicked it into the air with a quick movement of his foot, bounced it off his knees a few times, then his forehead. It was a performance, but one that came instinctively to him, full of litheness and skill. It was not the feat so much as the way it had been accomplished that immediately suggested an esoteric mastery.

'He's a great exhibitionist, that Corrente,' said Tozzi in a voice loud enough for the player to hear.

The boy gave a quick grin, bounced the ball on to the tiled floor like a basketball player, then led the way out.

I was relieved to see that Giacon had already moved on and was walking along the side of the stadium a hundred metres ahead of us, chatting to another of the Fiorentina players.

'That's modern football for you.' Tozzi jerked his chin towards some of the cars parked nearby, a nice clutch of powerful saloons and colourful two-seaters. 'I can remember having to attend training-sessions by courtesy of public transport. These boys today.' He grinned, Corrente grinned. Still very jolly. And it left me wondering why. There was more to the ploy than the obvious need to bind Corrente and myself together, to pave the way towards conversation. Tozzi's friendship with Corrente, the boy's admiration for the trainer – these I already knew.

'I was saying to Harry,' Corrente murmured, 'that he

105

looks fit for a journalist. A lot of them suffer too much from the easy life.'

'You haven't seen anything yet,' Tozzi joked. 'Wait until you see him training. That's right, Harry, no?'

'No,' I muttered, and Corrente stared at me with a quizzical smile on his face. I back-peddled quickly. 'The last time I kicked a football in anger, that was twelve, fifteen years ago. Don't expect too much either way.'

'We won't. The last time anyone did this one – a couple of years ago – we left him to crawl off exhausted after the first fifteen minutes. You remember him, Gianni, the German who thought our training methods were too slanted towards ball-control, not attentive enough with regard to fitness.' Tozzi looked back at me. 'We murdered him. But that was during pre-season training. Today it shouldn't be too bad.'

What I envisaged as a usual crowd had gathered inside the Campo Militare, the training pitch next door to the main stadium: old men sitting patiently on the steps of the concrete stand, youngsters pretending to be ball-jugglers, journalists talking to players, *massagiatori* putting up hurdles and marking out areas.

Off to one side one of the trainers was putting the three goalkeepers through their paces, slamming a football against the nearby walling, forcing them to turn at the last moment and make a clean catch. On the pitch itself another player was being forced to perform contortionist exercises, his body bending and swaying from side to side like a rubber band entwined in the fingers of a neurotic.

'Dino, I'll take Gianni with me,' I said. 'Just lapping the track gently. Nothing too strenuous.'

Tozzi looked uncertain but Corrente nodded, looked at me. I shrugged. We set off.

Gentle was the word for it, lightly kicking up the red cinders under our feet. I looked across after we had covered the first half of the lap and saw that the other players were

106

jogging round after us in pairs strung out into a long blue crocodile.

'He strikes me as being a kind man, that Tozzi,' I said to Corrente. 'How do you feel about him, Gianni?' I could sense the sweat beginning to break out on my skin, but otherwise comfortable enough.

'It's hard for us to make comparisons,' the boy replied. 'He's the only manager most of us have ever had close contact with. But he's very fair to all of us, seldom loses his temper even if we've played badly and deserve to have strips torn off us.'

'And you. Personally, I mean,' I said.

He looked across. 'He's never been angry towards me.'

'You've never noticed a sudden change in his attitude towards you?' I said.

'Of course. He feels very badly if I have a poor game, tells me that I'm the one responsible for ensuring the team's style of play.' He paused as we trotted past a clutch of spectators knotted together to one side of the track. 'The real change has come in the past day or two. He's been very friendly and solicitous recently. It's been embarrassing.'

'As far as the other players are concerned, you mean?'

'Partly that. But also the business of prying into my private life. What I do in the evenings, who I see. That kind of thing.' He paused. 'Has he told you about the letters?'

I literally pulled up in my tracks. He ran on, stopped, came back to where I was standing, hands on hips and making a great business of trying to look more breathless than I really was.

I shook my head, looked off across the width of the stadium. 'What letters?' I asked.

I could sense him looking at me intently, turned my head so that my eyes met his, classically uncertain and worried.

'Hell,' I said cheerfully. 'You may as well tell me now.

107

The chances are that in any case I'll find out soon enough, aren't they?'

The pack were closing up to us. Corrente took my arm. 'Let's run,' he said. He set off in a sprint, eased off to allow me a chance to catch up, told me the story of the threatening letters in a sense of panting urgency, as we continued to trot around the track.

It wasn't my lucky day. First the gentleman with the glass eye, now this. The story Corrente told me was at base the story I had been told by Tozzi and Regalia. No noticeable errors of omission or commission. But there was, of course, the one difference – that of Corrente's attitude in all this.

'You scared?' I asked.

'Of course,' the boy answered. 'After Tozzi spoke to me, I began to see that maybe the thing was more important than I realised. At first I just wanted to ignore the whole thing. I've had letters like this before.' He paused. 'For me it really is a problem. Look, Harry, my parents are poor, they come from the slums of Cagliari. I'm not a political animal at all; but deep down I have to admire these people for what they're trying to do. Is it such a bad thing to want to improve yourself?'

'A good thing,' I said, 'as long as you do it with an understanding of the meaning of dignity.'

'That,' Corrente said, 'that I think I've got. I don't know how you measure these things and perhaps I don't know how far you can measure them. Take my father. For the past three years I've been pressing him to move, to let me buy him a nice house somewhere in the *contado* just outside Cagliari. But no. He knows and loves his neighbours, he says, why should he move? So I buy my parents presents from time to time, put my money into banks and securities in the hope that one day I will be able to help them more. What can I do?'

'Continue to respect and love them,' I said. 'They sound the sort of people who know the meaning of dignity and

108

pride, who value affection and friendship very highly. You can't do more than to make sure you stay in one piece.'

His eyes flicked over my face nervously. 'You don't think it's that serious, all this panic.'

I smiled. 'Me, I'm just a poor journalist trying to do his job, good at languages, fairly fit, nothing more.'

He grinned, put a hand on my shoulder. 'Let's see how fit you really are,' he said, and began his jogging again.

I joined him and we both joined Tozzi and the other players.

There were inquisitive looks from some of them, introductions to others. But my mind was elsewhere. A conscientious bodyguard would have inspected every hurdle on the track for signs of tampering: run over the soles of every pair of football boots for evidence of loose studs, untidy nails; Holmes-like, would have scoured the ground for evidence of hanky-panky and malpractice; made absolutely certain that his body was at all times between the line of vision of the people in the stands and the subject to be guarded.

Me? Not me. All of a sudden I had come to the conclusion that it wouldn't have been worth the effort.

Instead I stuck close to Tozzi. He was nearer my age than anyone else on the field, a neat excuse not to involve myself in too much football and thus betray my essential ignorance of the subject.

14

We were in the changing-rooms, ninety minutes later.

The players had been put through their paces in a training game: no real tackling but a variation on touch-football. I couldn't help but be amazed at the way in which all the players concerned had a sleight of foot that made the impossible seem childishly easy. Corrente? He ambled about casually, stroking the ball through defensive gaps with the pinpoint accuracy of a target-shooter. Tozzi rushed about on one touchline yelping orders. He was harsh and unremitting towards those players who didn't appear to be taking the thing seriously enough. 'Stroke it, stroke it. You're stabbing. Easy, relaxed, don't get flustered.' He didn't swear or threaten but his messages were getting through. I scampered around in his wake, while he did his best to mutter a few asides in my direction. After the practice game, more exercises. And after the exercises, into the showers.

Again an unfamiliar scene. Steaming bodies, slicked-down hair. Off in the angle of the room one of the players was examining his genitals with the tender care of a dog licking his privates. Another player was on the massage table, his right thigh shivering under the attention of the *massagiatore* I'd seen earlier.

'Like that every time?' I asked Tozzi as we changed.

'Sometimes better, sometimes worse,' he replied. 'There are a million different attitudes towards training, but the only one that is laudable must be the one that gains the best results, brings the best out of the people you have to look after. Some managers, they have their players as fit as gladiators at the start of the season. Others like to take it gently, build it up gradually over a period of weeks, allow natural talent to predominate at the outset. The former run the risk of exhausting their players half-way through the season. The latter run the risk of getting into their stride too late. Me, I try to keep it steady, never over-work them simply because they've lost a game. It can be fatal to be inconsistent.' He shrugged. 'They're nice boys. But they're children. You have to treat them carefully.'

'Corrente seemed casual,' I said.

He smiled. 'He's the fittest player in the team, but he never has to prove it. The first time I saw him play he was seventeen and passing the ball like a pin-table expert. Beautiful control, the control of a born ball-player. Then you add his intelligence and you have something special. You know, he plays football like a chess grandmaster, moves ahead of the rest of the people on the field. Football-ers don't fall over for no reason at all, but when Gianni's on song the players in the opposing defences sometimes appear like lead-bottom soldiers, wobbling and swaying this way and that, so often wrong-footed by a move he's made. He's a bloody genius. Watch him carefully. You won't see many better. Pele, Rivera, Di Stefano, Bobby Charlton, Beckenbauer, Maradonà, they've been some of the great instinctual players of modern football. Give Gianni a couple of years and he'll be seen to be good enough to quote in that company.'

'If he lives that long,' I said cheerlessly.

'You can't talk about danger and death like that!'

Privately I agreed. It was a callous, an untypical, uncharacteristic remark to make, and I knew it. But it served to get Tozzi away from his football romanticisms and back to pragmatic realities.

'Just tell me how to play this thing from now on. Now that the problem is immediate, no longer a flimsy idea. My guess is that Regalia will have Corrente tailed by one, even two men for the next few days. In usual circumstances, the ones that are totally unusual, you need a posse of agents sliding around like the images in a tryptical mirror. But Corrente's movements must be fairly standard, no?'

'He has a flat in the Borgo San Jacopo right here in town. Very central, just across the river from the Uffizi, very high rent but he never wants for money.'

'And his private life?' I asked casually.

Tozzi shot me a quick look, then shrugged. 'Nothing extraordinary, I think. Likes girls; likes to gamble a little; reads a lot, mostly *gialli*, detective novels; goes to the cinema; drinks occassionally when he visits discotheques and nightclubs. The usual things. But you must remember that even here, where things are not over-regimented, we use the system of *ritiro* before and after matches.'

'*Ritiro?*' I said.

'Just a precaution. We'll call the players together for, say, two nights and a day before an important match. Get them to bed early, make sure that they eat well, have an opportunity to relax. Even then it's hell for some players who can't bear to be away from wives and children. They spend their whole time plaguing the switchboard with calls for home. Corrente doesn't have that problem.'

'You'll be doing that before the next match?' I asked. 'Putting everyone into *ritiro*?'

'Of course. Just for a couple of days.'

'Till then, I think it would be a good idea for you to stay close to him, Tozzi,' I said. 'There are still some things I want to find out, people I want to talk to.'

He began to look anxious, but I cut him off.

'You've got Regalia's people,' I pointed out. 'And you've got your common sense. Stay close to the boy when you're in the open, say when you're moving out of a car and into a building. Regalia's no fool. He'll look after you. And I'll be around as much as I can.'

He nodded, and Corrente came into the room from the

113

showers, looking clean and fresh. He gave me a quick smile, began to get dressed.

'Are you busy this evening, Gianni?' Tozzi asked.

The boy looked up, began to worry at his top lip with his lower teeth, then shook his head. 'Unless there's something you'd like me to do.'

Tozzi nodded at me. 'I thought perhaps we could go to a club, have a few drinks together, give Harry a taste of Florentine night-life. Nothing special.' He paused. 'You needn't if you don't want to.'

Corrente untoothed his lip, gave a nervous smile. He said, 'Fine,' without sounding confident that he meant it. He mentioned the name of a club, Tozzi threw another back at him, they haggled, Corrente won. He looked pleased that he'd won. Tozzi looked annoyed that he hadn't won. I couldn't perceive the importance of the victory. As far as I was concerned a nightclub was a nightclub, was an excuse to pay too much for alcohol, a place where the girls serving the stuff usually had hair like candyfloss, eyes like pellets of black onyx and thighs with telltale bruises. I never yet found a damn thing in one of those places that I would want to remember on the morning after the night before.

I arranged to turn up at the given nightclub at eight, walked out of the dressing-room with them, stood patiently by while they discussed the practice-session with the clutch of journalists outside.

Giacon came up to me, gave a sly wink and then offered congratulations on my apparent fitness. 'You magazine people,' he said with a smile. 'You dictate your stuff to some leggy secretary while sweating away on a rowing-machine.' But the wink and the smile had been utterly humourless, the words utterly meaningless, both gestures of a man close to something worth being close to.

I saw Tozzi and Corrente to the latter's green Porsche, watched as a grey Alfa saloon with no markings and two passengers followed in its wake, walked quickly away to where Spezia was waiting in our Croma, his face a mask of imperturbability.

I slipped into the passenger seat and transferred the Beretta from my pocket to its rightful hiding-place.

'The hotel,' I said to Spezia as he pulled the car into the middle of the road. 'And when you've dropped me, go home and collect your toothbrush. We're moving you into the Excelsior at a million lire a night, my friend. This thing's starting to get out of hand.'

I looked at him as I spoke, but it was a waste of time. He looked about as excited as a whore talking to one of her customers on a busy *cinq-à-sept*.

15

I RANG REGALIA as soon as I had reached my room and checked it out.

I have always detested the impersonality of telephone conversations. In a trade where watchfulness counts for so much it is castrating to be denied the sight of the face one is addressing. Everything seems so two-dimensional. But I had reasons for not wanting another conference in Regalia's office.

Regalia sounded surprised to hear from me. I couldn't understand why. After all he had asked me to contact him frequently.

'No news on Mimmi, then,' I said.

'Nothing.' He didn't sound at all cheerful.

'It'll come,' I said.

'Never mind that,' he replied. 'Tell me about yourself.'

'Nothing much,' I murmured.

'No bullets and knives? You surprise me. What happened to that animal magnetism of yours.'

'Ha, ha,' I said. 'Tell me about the girl.'

'What girl?'

'You know damn well what girl.'

'Ah, that girl.'

'That girl. Tell me everything.'

Paper rustled at the other end of the line. Regalia's voice became formal.

'Soffici, Guiliana,' he said. 'Born 2nd April, 1967 here in Florence. Height: one metre, sixty-eight; weight: fifty-three kilos. That's about all I can tell you.'

'And Corrente?' I asked. 'How long have they known each other?'

'For God's sake, Mann,' he rasped. 'This isn't a bloody police state.'

'A joke, that,' I said.

'*Porcamadonna*,' he muttered. 'We've only known about her for a matter of hours and we've only got a limited number of records to turn to. Give us a chance. Just one, that's all we ask.' I held the receiver away as he muttered threats and issued expletives.

'So how many men have you got on Corrente?' I asked.

'Is he there with you?'

'Of course he isn't,' I snapped. 'I saw only two. That boy I bumped into in your office yesterday and one other.'

'What the hell are they paying you for, then?'

'How many, Regalia? Dammit, you tell me or I'll cross the square and take you apart.'

He laughed.

I laughed.

'Two on his house,' he continued, 'two on Tozzi's house so that he's covered if Tozzi prefers to have him under his own roof. And when I say have, don't take it the wrong way.'

'No evidence of homosexuality?' I said.

He gave me a quick sermon on idiocy, then became serious.

'It's not a completely crazy question,' he said. 'In this particular case, yes; in general, no. You can sense it sometimes as far as some of the journalists are concerned in the manner in which they write their reports. And often the homosexual interest may assert itself in terms of hatred rather than affection. There's one powerful journalist here who cannot stand Corrente's play at any price. While all the other newspapers are praising the boy's genius, this character does little more than give a metaphorical nod of encouragement, usually accuses him of sloth, of being too clever for his own good.'

'Who's that?' I asked, but I was ready for the answer before I'd spoken.

'A man called Angelo Giacon, works for the local paper here.'

'I met him this afternoon,' I said.

'So?'

'He was very polite towards both Tozzi and Corrente.'

'Of course, of course. This attitude I'm talking about is subtle. Football is as much a way of life for him as it is for any manager or player. He can't be overt or blatant in his criticisms, particularly in view of the fact that Tozzi is one of the successful managers in the game, Corrente a player of some genius. But over a period of time the picture gradually becomes clear, when following game after game Giacon's comments about the boy are less enthusiastic than those of other commentators. You reach a point at which athletic and tactical considerations appear irrelevant and you're left merely with a veiled attempt at character assassination. The veneer of politeness is always there between these people, but you would never see Tozzi or Corrente voting for Giacon in a Journalist of the Year poll.'

'Tell me more?'

'About whom? Giacon?'

'Of course Giacon,' I said. 'Who did you think I meant?'

'You're taking this seriously, but you're forgetting one thing,' he growled.

'What's that?'

'I'm the man who asks the questions and questions the answers. You, you're the man whose job is just neat and functional.'

'Wrong,' I said. 'I do the question and answer bit myself before I really get down to work. Tell me about Giacon.'

'Nothing much to tell. Comes from Piacenza, fairly normal education, did very well during his national service, became something of a crack-shot in rifle practice and went into competitions for the army. When he left he turned to journalism, worked for a time on the *Corriere della Sera* in

119

Milan, then was sent down here by them. Five, six years ago transferred on to the local paper here.'

'Age?'

'Yours or mine.'

'No wife?' I asked.

'No wife. No children that we know of.'

'Very funny,' I said.

'Mistresses aren't exactly rare in Italy, Mann. But Giacon seems to eschew the idea of that sort of liaison as well.'

'Lives where?'

'Flat somewhere near the stadium. Via Cimabue, I think.'

'I thought you said this wasn't a police state,' I said.

'And you said my saying that was a joke.'

'Damn right, wasn't I?'

'Could be, couldn't you?'

'A nosey man, Giacon,' I said to get him back on course.

'Very nosey, very smart, very perceptive. He's not a man you can fool easily. And mistakes you made this afternoon, he'll be putting two and two together and coming up with three. And he won't love you too much for your connection with Corrente. You'll see him again, my friend. Be sure of that.'

'Will he tell me?' I asked.

'If he comes to the right conclusion, you mean?' He paused. 'I think so. He's vain, very vain. He'll want you to know that he knows what no-one is supposed to know.'

I began to wind up the conversation, then realised that there was something I'd forgotten.

'Do me a favour?' I asked.

'What favour?'

I gave him the number of the Lancia Thema, wondered aloud and gently whether he could give me the name of the owner.

'It'll take a few minutes,' he said.

'No hurry,' I said.

120

I thanked him, didn't answer his query as to my intended movements, and hung up.

I showered, changed into a fresh shirt and lay down on the bed.

Fifteen minutes later Spezia was back with paper suitcase and blank expression.

I checked him into a room on the same floor and a few units away, gave him time to relax for a few minutes. And then we were away again to see Belmonte's wife.

16

THE GREEN FIAT was parked where it had been on our visit that morning. Alongside it was another car, but not the one I might remotely have expected.

'Could be fun,' I said to Spezia as we drew to a halt.

He nodded. 'If you don't mind my saying so, I thought you handled that one badly.'

'I didn't realise you saw it,' I said.

'That and the training session,' he said. 'You trained very nicely, but the earlier – that not so nicely.'

'Hell,' I said. 'Now's when we find out how important all that was.' I climbed out of the car, spoke to Spezia again before closing the door. 'Move the car round so that you're blocking them both.'

He nodded.

'It may be that this is just a little social call that our friend's making,' I continued. 'If so, you can always move. If not, it could be useful that we stop him leaving in a hurry.'

I ambled across the gravel and up the stairs, but I never needed the chance to tinkle the collection of metal tubes a second time. The door beside them was a few centimetres ajar.

I whipped the Beretta out of its holster, transferred it to the right pocket of my jacket, wrapped my right hand round the butt to keep it company and pushed the door open with my shoulder and the fingers of my left hand.

As I did so there was a clicking noise from somewhere

inside the villa, followed by the pad of feet on the soft-pile carpeting.

Legs appeared on the spiral staircase, the feet dressed in woollen slippers, then a floral dressing-gown, finally the handsome head of Signora Linda Belmonte.

Her hair was unkempt, most of the lipstick had been wiped of her mouth, the make-up at the periphery of her blue eyes was smudged, the eyes themselves profoundly unhappy. They jerked from my face to the stairs to my face again like those of an animal trapped by two counter forces.

'The door was open,' I said gruffly. 'I let myself in.'

Before she had either the time or the inclination to reply, more feet appeared on the spiral staircase, swathed in soft black leather, the legs and lower torso wrapped in light-grey slacks. He was bare from the waist upwards, the black hair across his flat chest and stomach forming a T-shape, the arms not strongly muscled but still wide at the wrist. A gold crucifix hung from the gold chain round his neck; as though he knew the first thing about the humanism of religious belief. He was still wearing his fancy dark glasses.

Linda Belmonte said, 'What do you want, Signor Mann?' Her voice was soft, a strangulated whisper; not the voice of outrage.

'I just wanted to talk,' I said. 'To ask some questions. It appears I came at the wrong time.'

She didn't move, either to acknowledge my statement or to hint at my leaving.

'Your friend,' I said. I jerked my head up. Her eyes were on mine, close to tears. 'We've met before but we didn't introduce ourselves properly.'

She snapped her eyes towards him, back towards me. 'Harry Mann. And this is Giuseppe Fosso.'

He looked terribly casual, the lower part of his face completely relaxed. He gave a quick smirk. 'If you don't mind, Linda and I have some unfinished business to attend to.'

I might have left, but for his next move. His right hand

124

came up and to rest on her left shoulder, a gesture that was simultaneously intended to be casual and authoritative, a clear indication of the proprietorial power he exercised over her.

She tried hard to control herself, to appear at ease, but the flinching movement was there in the way in which her body tautened. And it was enough to decide me.

'Don't be ridiculous,' I said tightly. 'The last time I came to the villa I was given a mass of non-information. The last time I saw you, you damn nearly stuck a knife into my belly. Don't think this time I'm going to walk away from here like an ingenuous idiot. There could be too much at stake. It's not your house, and inside it I'm not about to be pushed around by some devious gigolo on the make.' I paused and looked at Linda Belmonte. 'I'll go, but when the lady tells me to go and not before.'

Nice speech. On the heavy side, perhaps, but nice enough. The trouble was his nudity. He had no gun or knife that I could see, and our earlier meetings had suggested a character eager to play rough when the occasion demanded. His lack of armament made him a man very aware of his power, prepared to bivouac behind the protection the woman might be able to afford him, and unlikely to fall prey to bluff.

He shrugged, came down the remaining two steps on to the floor of the hallway. 'Linda,' he said the word as though unaccustomed to it, 'tell him to leave.'

She looked at me for a long moment, lifted her head, nodded, looked away quickly.

'Please go away,' she said. Her voice was off-key. 'We don't really have anything to discuss.'

I thought otherwise, but given the set of circumstances there seemed little likelihood of getting any further information out of either of them for the time being.

I nodded, began to move away, and then heard something that made me stop. I looked across at the two of them. They had also heard it and were both rigid, statu-esque in their aural concentration.

I flicked the Beretta out of my pocket and its barrel in their direction.

The noise of a car engine, of its wheels on the gravel of the driveway, grew louder and more distinct. Not the engine of a small car but the throbbing purr of something that sounded powerful and commanding.

'I'll just delay my departure a few moments,' I said grimly. 'That is, if you don't mind.'

The smirk had been wiped clean off the lower part of Fosso's face. As for the woman, hers had come apart at the seams, the eyes staring maniacally past me towards the doorway behind.

17

THERE WAS A brief moment when time hung heavily in the air like a dark cloud, when the voices from outside sounded harshly blurred like the noise of a record being played at half-speed. And then he came in, the owner of the house and chief breadwinner, Commendatore Giorgio Belmonte.

He threw the door open energetically, marched in, did a grotesque double-take as he saw the gun in my hand, the half-naked figure of Fosso on the stairway, and his brown face became darkened with blood.

He looked at each of us in turn, his eyes finally coming to rest on mine as they flicked about from one to another of the fraternity.

'What the hell – ' he began, but I cut him off.

'Nothing to do with me, Belmonte,' I said. I waved him further into the room with the gun. 'I came out for a nice quiet talk with your wife and found this.'

As Belmonte shuffled along the hallway, I looked across at his wife. Where a few moments earlier her face had epitomised misery, it had now acquired a strange flush, the light-blue eyes bright and proud, focused on those of her husband. And the hands that had formerly clutched the edges of the dressing-gown closely round her body had fallen away, exposing her semi-nakedness, bra and panties black and silken with genteel frills at the edges. The flesh was slightly slack over hips and across stomach but there was no mistaking the sexuality that her body had to offer.

The expression on Belmonte's face hardened and became enraged. But there was a strangely marionettish quality to his movements and gestures. It was as though his thought-processes had been pre-programmed, as though this was a situation that he had foreseen at some earlier moment, or in some remembered dream, perhaps not in detail but certainly as to essence and the attitudes expressed.

Like a bad actor in a low-budget soap opera he walked over to his wife and spat on to the floor by her slippered feet.

'*Macche putana*,' he shouted. He began to shake with simulated rage. 'You whoring bitch. I picked you out of the gutter, you and that bastard child of yours. I got rid of the child for you, gave you wealth and respectability by marrying you when I needn't have bothered. And this is what you do to me.' His right hand swung round, flat and hard on to her left cheek, snapping her head to one side.

Gentle recoil brought it back to centre and it was worth watching. The left side of her face was pinkened and baby-bright, but her eyes were harsh and bleak, mad with rage.

'You hypocritical bastard,' she hissed. Her voice was low, full of venom. 'What the hell have you done with your life except chase other women, leave me here by myself? God only knows, if I'd had as many lovers as you I'd be a wrinkled old hag by now.' She began to shake her shoulders, brought her hands up to pull the robe off. It fell to the floor in a sad pile behind her. 'The first lover I've ever taken, and you can't take it, can you?' Her hands and lower arms were out of sight behind her back. 'I find someone who can appreciate my body,' she continued, 'the first person in twenty years, and you can't take it.' Her brassiere loosened, then fell away to reveal firm breasts.

'Stop it, you slut,' Belmonte yelled and I put a bullet no more than a few centimetres away from Fosso's head.

It was a good time to call a halt to the striptease – being a fly on the wall during matrimonial skirmishes is not my line of business. But the real reason lay with Dead-Eye. Throughout the performance currently being exhibited by the Belmonte family, Fosso had been edging his way around on the stairway preparatory to making a run for the bedroom upstairs.

'Don't move, my friend,' I said to him. He had frozen into statuesque immobility, a near-laughable figure. 'The next one will be closer.'

Linda Belmonte looked at me with unfocused eyes.

'Get dressed, signora,' I said. 'I want to leave the house but I'm damned if I'll do it while you three are in this mood. Go up and get dressed.'

She was listening now, still half-crazed, but those eyes were concentrating on mine.

'While you're upstairs, you can bring down his clothes.' I nodded in the direction of Fosso. 'Sorry to break up the party, signora, but it seems to me you and your husband have things to talk over. Two's company, and on occasions such as these any number that's greater only serves to smudge the argument.'

Her eyes were in gear again now. She nodded, picked up her brassiere and the dressing-gown, brushed past Fosso and climbed out of sight.

'Sorry about the damage, Belmonte,' I said. 'But you can always send me the bill if you ever feel like pressing the point.'

He was looking lost. He had programmed his actions, remembered his lines and now he found himself left without a script from which to work. He didn't even seem particularly interested in Fosso, in fact was not even looking in his direction.

Silence grew again, smeared only by the muffled sounds of footsteps from the floor above. A door opened, slammed closed and Fosso's clothes tumbled down the well of the stairway. They fell on to the floor with a hollow soft sound. No gun. That had been my only worry.

'Pick them up, get dressed and no bizarre movements,' I said. I kept the Beretta on him while he did that.

Belmonte's wife appeared again, wearing a satin sleeveless dress in royal blue, matching shoes and hair that had been brushed out of its former disarray. I'd seen them all before earlier in the day. She stopped at the bottom of the stairway, then slowly walked over to Belmonte, put her hands on the sides of his head and stared at him. It was a gesture of extreme tenderness, one he was incapable of understanding. She took her hands away, her arms fell to her sides and she turned towards me.

'I came to ask some questions, signora,' I said. 'Perhaps now I have some of the answers. I don't know for sure.'

She shrugged. 'It doesn't matter. Please leave. Giorgio and I have things to discuss.'

'You'll be all right?' I asked.

She smiled. 'Of course. Why not? All this needs is a bit of honesty, saying things that we have forgotten how to say.'

I nodded, looked across at Fosso, gestured him towards the door with the gun.

Belmonte's face was still blank and unknowing. He didn't even seem capable of grasping the essential truth of the whole affair – that he had married a woman with a self-knowledge and honesty that deserved trust and respect, someone who made him appear desperately two-dimensional.

I saw Fosso to his car, made Spezia move so that he could manoeuvre his sleek Lancia. There was nothing for either of us to say. He knew my game and I knew his, and we both knew that we would meet again. I watched the car all the way down the drive.

And then I took in the most recent automobile addition to the private motor show that had been taking place outside the villa. It was the car I'd seen outside my hotel, a lemon-coloured Volvo 740GL Grand Luxe. Distance covered to date was a mere nine thousand kilometres. That made it a first-rate car, already proven, with the promise of much more smooth motoring to come.

I told Spezia the whys and wherefores of the episode in the villa as we drove back to town and he grumbled again.

'Seems to me you didn't handle *that* one too well either,' he said.

'Oh hell,' I said, and I thought he grinned. I couldn't be sure. But the lower part of his face had appeared to give a quick twitch.

18

THE CLUB AT which I had arranged to meet Tozzi and Corrente was tucked in a side-street just off the lower part of the Via Tornabuoni, advertised with neon lighting in pastel shades of pink, blue and yellow that would have made a zebra feel underdressed.

In the main road the whores were out in force, being baited by troups of cowards leaning out of over-packed cars, giving back as good as they got.

I left Spezia and the car a few yards down the street and made my back to the nightclub. Underneath the signs outside were glossy prints of the evening's star attraction, an artiste who went under the sobriquet of *Stella Pratti*. Even the harshness of the lighting and over-use of the make-up box couldn't disguise the fact that the picture bore a close resemblance to that of Giuliana Soffici, the girl with whom I had seen Corrente the previous day.

I wandered into the lobby, was jumped on by an official wearing fancy-dress, given the privilege of being made a club member and made my way down burgundy-carpeted steps into the bar at the mezzanine level.

Tozzi and Corrente were sitting on low stools at a small table in one corner of the bar. Not more than five metres away from them at another table were two fresh-faced youngsters in grey suits, white shirts and boring ties looking as out of place in the environment as a pair of monks at a blue-film show.

As I appeared in the entrance-way they made a great fuss of finishing their drinks, putting cigarette packets and lighters into coat pockets and looking intensely at one another.

I waited for them to leave, checked an impulse to congratulate them on the extreme subtlety of their cover, and went over to Corrente and Tozzi.

I ordered my usual Riccadonna on ice, stuck my legs out in front of me and tried to look as nonchalant as possible.

'They weren't good, were they, Harry?' Corrente said. His smile was relaxed.

'Not good at all,' I said. 'Who's been telling you what?'

I looked across at Tozzi. He was back to midday form, looking a professional misery. He jerked his head up in my direction as my question went in that of Corrente.

'No-one had to tell me anything, Harry,' Corrente said easily. 'They were just so obvious all the time. The Alfa followed us all the way to Dino's flat. I looked out of the window at one point while Dino was making a quick telephone call and they were still there. They were there when we left to come here, they arrived here only a few seconds after we did and didn't say a word to each other, just sat and stared at the floor. They didn't even look at us, which was silly of them, don't you think? It got me thinking.'

I shrugged. 'Must be police,' I said. 'Those suits, the quietness, all the patient shadowing.'

'Can't be anything to do with those letters, then.'

'There's that,' I said. 'But these people can't be on the other side. Not the right sort of style for that.' I paused, turned to Tozzi. 'You know what it's all about, Dino?' I asked.

Tozzi's head, lined with self-doubt, swung from side to side. He hadn't said anything since I'd arrived.

'The club knows about the letters, Gianni,' I said to the boy. 'Maybe someone there thought it might be useful for you to be covered until this thing dies down. One of the directors, perhaps, maybe more than one. You represent a

134

fair amount of their financial interest and they must have good contacts with the *Pubblica Sicurezza* and the *Carabiniere*. They don't want to take risks and can easily arrange for some form of police cover.'

Corrente nodded slowly and calmly. A toothpick was juggling around energetically at one corner of his mouth. He prised it out, broke it in two with the fingers of his right hand, looked at me firmly.

'I'm still here, Harry,' he said.

I raised my eyebrows. 'So?'

'So, why aren't those two still here doing their job of looking after me?'

I shook my head. 'Search me,' I said. 'Perhaps they've gone to have a pee. Perhaps they're queer. Perhaps they've gone to phone into headquarters.'

'Or perhaps,' Corrente said, 'they knew that once you'd arrived, they'd be free to take a rest.'

'Meaning?' I asked.

'I'm sorry, Harry,' Corrente said calmly. 'You don't fool me a bit.'

I made a great fuss of lighting a cigarette and taking a gulp from my drink. And at the end of that Corrente's eyes were still looking in my direction.

'Two things, Harry,' he said. 'First there was the scar in the small of your back. I saw that while we were changing this afternoon. You were talking to Dino, your back was turned to me.'

'Anything unusual about it?' I asked. 'People fall down, have accidents.'

'They don't fall down backwards on to bullets, Harry,' he said. 'I've been to the cinema many times. And that looked to me like a bullet-scar.'

'Fair enough,' I said. 'And the other thing?'

'The gun, Harry.'

He leant towards me. His left hand patted the right-hand pocket of my jacket. 'Well,' he said. 'It was there this

135

afternoon, or something like that, something of that weight and size.'

I stared at him. Guns are a damn nuisance, or rather, concealing them can be. They can be a nuisance in other respects, also.

I shrugged. 'So now you've guessed.'

He nodded, then gave a quick smile. 'You were too good this afternoon, you know. Too fast and strong with that powerful physique of yours. I've only been in this game a comparatively short time but I've never yet met a journalist who looked as fit as you do. It got me thinking. That and Giacon.'

'Giacon?' I couldn't keep the anger out of my voice.

'Of course. He's a bitch, a male bitch. But he's smart. And before I'd even met you, just before I arrived for training he told me that he didn't think you rang true in the guise of a journalist.'

'The bastard,' I muttered.

'Oh, he was clever,' Corrente said. 'I couldn't understand it. He normally avoids me on these occasions, never gives me a good write-up unless I've played really well. There he was, his hand on my shoulder, almost whispering to me. I couldn't understand it,' he repeated. 'But it set me thinking, Harry.'

I nodded, looked at Tozzi. Still miserable.

The hell with him, I thought. So I gave Corrente the story, at least those parts of the story as they pertained to him. How I'd been asked to do a job, the terms of reference, the need to keep the facts from him.

He listened calmly, waited for me to finish.

'It's always the same,' he said. 'Always they treat us like *bambini*. Of course, as a breed we deserve it. But sometimes, just once or twice, I wish they'd treat us like adults.' He patted Tozzi on the knee, gave him a warm smile. '*Eh*, Dino?'

Tozzi mumbled a platitudinous apology.

Corrente looked at me. 'So we have you to look after us, Harry. I'm glad. I think I like you.'

'It's the scar in the middle of the back, my friend,' I said. 'It lights up when it comes face to face with someone it likes.'

He grinned, looked at the thin gold watch strapped to his left wrist. 'Let's go inside,' he said. 'We may as well relax and enjoy ourselves now the air's been cleared.'

He stood up, clenched and relaxed the fingers of his left hand a few times, then led the way through a doorway to one side of the bar.

19

THE ROOM WAS a mixture of chic and cavern. There was bogus plasterwork decoration on ceiling and walls. The floor was covered with heavy carpeting in the standard burgundy colouring I had already noticed.

Comfortable-looking chairs with armrests lay in semi-circular formations round marble-topped tables. The only lights in the room came from dim lamps in the centre of each table. The chairs all faced in the direction of a small stage tucked on to one plane of the room.

As we came in a talentless tenor was bawling his way through the last few words of a heavily-sentimental ballad about some girl called Lola who didn't appear to have been very interested in what he had to offer. Instead of looking disheartened the character on stage was beaming with the happiness of a demented lover. Small applause as he bellowed the final notes. Small wonder.

Curtains came down over the stage, the amplifier system gave us a sickly orchestral pot-pourri of current hit tunes, the lighting went up and a smooth character in a snappy dark suit showed us to a table, not far enough from the stage to cause eye-strain, not close enough so that we might be able to smell the grease-paint.

We sat down and ordered drinks.

'The next performer,' Corrente said to me from the left. 'That's the reason for the visit.' His eyes were bright with expectancy.

'Stella Pratti?' I asked innocently.

'You know of her?' Corrente asked excitedly.

I shook my head. 'Just the teasers outside the front door.'

'Ah,' he said. But he was still sitting close to the edge of his chair.

I turned to Tozzi. 'And you, Dino,' I said. 'You know of this girl?'

He mumbled something to the effect that he thought he might have heard of her. Misery Tozzi still. And his answer couldn't help but sound pathetically phony.

Very sharply the music switched off, the lights on each table simultaneously dimmed, then went out and the room was plunged into complete darkness.

Out of instinct my hand was digging towards the Beretta, the need for utter caution screaming in my mind. Too late I realised that I had made the wrong move: tiredness, perhaps. But I needn't have been bothered by the darkness, for a large disc of brightness suddenly cut into the room from a spotlight behind us, its diameter almost engrossing the area of the small stage, completely illuminating the person standing upon it.

She was breathtaking. Clever cosmetic work had rounded out the thinness of her features, had given her face a hard, almost pug-sexy, look that was artificial but yet alluring. The honey-blonde hair was waved and immaculately styled, falling on to her shoulders in languid curves. In the brightness of the spotlight it had taken on a doll-like pallidity that contrasted sharply with the high colour-tones of her flesh.

She was wearing a long sleeveless dress in emerald satin, cut low into a sharp cleavage and tight across stomach, hips and thighs. Her leisure clothes of the previous day had struck me as being a neat amalgam of the functional and the elegant, clothes of a person very much able to adapt to modern fashions to suit taste and personal idiosyncrasy. The dress she was wearing now was artificial, self-conscious, almost a throwback to Rita Hayworth and the era of the lavish Hollywood pot-boilers. And beneath the hem of the dress were matching slippers with pencil-thin heels.

Her left arm was thrown upwards and outwards, an unsubtle invitation to audience applause, which duly echoed forth. Her right arm was held close to her body, the fingers holding a pencil-microphone.

The instant the canned background music came on, she was off on a foot-tapping number about the boy she thought didn't love her, but not to worry, she'd been wrong all the time and really he did. It was a small, distinctive voice with no magical timbre underlying it, and little evidence of an ability to cover a wide range of notes.

I snatched a quick glance at my companions. Corrente was lighting a cigarette, the first time I'd seen him smoke. His face was flooded with naïve pleasure, his eyes glued fixedly on the girl.

In contrast to Corrente's edge-of-the-chair expectancy, Tozzi was slumped back in his seat, his face still pleasantly miserable. Some people, it seemed, made a fetish of being unhappy. But he was watching the girl no less attentively than Corrente. Same interest, it seemed. But different attitudes.

I drank, the room stared, the girl sang. More foot-tapping material, one or two ballads, all short and to the point, whatever it might have been. Me, it missed by several kilometres.

Then suddenly the mood changed. It was heralded by the near-disappearance of the microphone, the flex whipped upwards out of sight so that both the girl's hands were free and the microphone itself was suspended just above head-height and upside-down.

The move was the signal for strident applause, cries of 'Vai, vai,' a few obscenities, a few brief jokes which gave birth to harsh laughter from some of the nearby tables.

Corrente's face was now anxious, tight around the mouth and eyes, as though he was on the verge of an angry outburst.

The light on the stage grew smaller in diameter, now barely covered the girl's height. And the music that came

141

out over the loudspeaker was nothing more or less than old-fashioned bump and grind.

The words that went with the music were cheerfully obscene, no longer the lyrics to weak-spined ballads and secondhand hits. These words were a mass of innuendo and *double-entendre*, the story of a policeman who rode pillion on a scooter belonging to a nun. Nuns, priests and policemen have provided perennial targets for Italian humorous stories. But this was something else.

So was the girl. I should have expected something zany as soon as I had heard the bawdy remarks and got the hang of the licentious lyrics, but the striptease act came as a surprise. Hell, how can a stripper operate when she's wearing a dress that appears glued to her skin? I was still trying to puzzle the thing out when the girl's right hand went to the clasp of the dress across the lower point of her cleavage, ran slowly down over her flat belly and down to her crutch. Just a simple zip, cunningly camouflaged.

Her hands came up, caught the edges of the cleavage, down the length of her arms. She stepped out of the dress, kicked it behind her. Not for a moment had she stopped singing.

There were emerald-green tassles at the nipples of each breast, an emerald stud in her navel, a wispy green G-string where it should have been and where most of the populace obviously wished it absent or invisible.

Piercing whistles arrowed into the atmosphere from various parts of the room. There were further obscenities, more cries of '*vai, vai,*' and urgent pleas to keep the show moving as fast as possible to its predestined conclusion.

The naval stud was the obvious candidate for priority removal. The girl gingerly scooped it out with forefinger and thumb, lovingly took it up towards her mouth like someone savouring the last member of a box of chocolates, kissed it lasciviously, licking it before tossing it into the crowd.

More cries, more whistles, more commands.

For a few moments came the routine tassel-swinging act as the upper part of the girl's torso swung convulsively from side to side, the small breasts and their appendages swirling in ever-faster circumferences. Having been overtly fondled, the latter in turn made their way into the crowd.

Suddenly the music snapped to a halt. For the space of a second the girl stared pointedly in the direction of our table, a tight smile pushing at the corners of her mouth. Then her hands went slowly down, over her breasts, across her ribs towards her hips, and the room was blanketed into darkness.

I slammed my arms outward to left and right, felt the bodies of both my companions jerk away off balance. My mind registered a flat whirring noise that cut past my right side and the world became a jumble of sharp impressions like a cinema reel being shuttled through an old projector.

In the split-second after the spotlight came on I looked at the girl. She was standing where she had been before, the G-string now missing. The knife had entered her body almost at the horizontal and only millimetres below her navel. It had buried itself hard to the hilt, making a flat smack of sound as it stopped fast.

The girl's eyes had snapped open and were staring ahead in a mixture of mystification and pain. Then her eyelids closed as she began to stumble backwards in the orgasm of agony. Her knees bent forward and sideways, her head slumped forward, her hair cascaded over her shoulders, her arms fell flat against her flanks as she slumped to the floor.

I ignored Corrente and Tozzi as they tried to pick themselves off the floor and swirled out of my chair to look behind me.

People were shouting, jumping out of their seats. Two bouncers at the edge of the back wall were pushing their way towards the stage. I wrestled my way past them, ran into the bar area. It was empty. So was the foyer. I turned and ran back into the main hall. Leaving Corrente and Tozzi had been strictly not according to the textbook. But

143

I had had to take the chance that the murderer was still in the house.

Pandemonium had broken out, with bouncers and waiters clawing their way towards the girl through crowds of spectators trying to get out. One was making his way to the main entrance, but his attempts to prevent people from leaving were feckless. He pushed down the first person to reach him, in turn had to give way to weight of numbers.

Corrente was on the verge of going berserk by the time I reached the table. All the implications of the murder must have been racing through his brain like the war-cries of the Furies.

I grabbed his arm and twisted it round viciously. 'There's nothing you can do, Gianni,' I yelled. 'We're leaving.'

He struggled wildly for a few moments, his wounded eyes jerking from my face to the stage, then went limp.

I grabbed Tozzi with my other hand.

'Get moving, Dino,' I said. 'You can't afford to become involved in this, and you know it.'

I bundled them past the prostrate bouncer, through the bar and foyer, along the street outside and into the back seat of the car.

'Move, and quick,' I shouted to Spezia. And the car was rolling as I pulled myself into the front passenger seat.

20

SPEZIA SLAMMED THE car towards the end of the narrow street, cleverly squeezing a way between the parked vehicles on one side and the high pavement on the other.

We turned right into the Via Porta Santa Maria, the road that leads down to the Ponte Vecchio, turned left at the bridge and sped eastwards along the north bank of the river.

Just as we went into the chicane by the Uffizi he murmured. 'We have someone with us.'

'Sure?' I asked.

He nodded.

The Fiat Crona has front and back windows nearly the width of the car but I ordered Corrente and Tozzi to get as low in the back seat as possible and to stay wide towards the sides.

'Just to make positive,' I said to Spezia, 'take us out of the centre of town. We'll have a good look at him.'

'Fiesole?' he asked.

'It'll do nicely,' I said. 'Lots of tricky bends on that road, and there shouldn't be too many cars on it at this time of the evening.'

We rocketed along the riverbank, took the big avenue that leads north from a point just east of the Ponte San Niccolo and shuttled over the railway tracks, up past the football stadiums and neighbouring swimming-pool.

'Still there?' I asked Spezia.

He nodded. 'All this may be a lot of nothing,' he said

bitterly. 'But right now I wish the back of my head was bullet-proof.'

'That's up to you, isn't it, chum?' I said.

He was driving beautifully, slipping through the gears with perfect timing of clutch and accelerator. It's not impossible to become a good driver. To be absolutely first-class you need more than merely the razor-sharp reactions. You also need the knowledge of an ace mechanic. Spezia was a boy with full qualifications on every side.

We swung sharply to the left at the end of the Viale Ojetti, made our way along a straight that lasted some nine hundred metres, cornered right and moved northward on the road that led to Fiesole.

I turned round to have a look at Corrente and Tozzi. The former had tears in his eyes; the latter was staring morosely out of the window. They were both too shocked to register genuine fright, were still locked in a private world to which I didn't have a means of access. There was nothing I could do for them except to make sure that they each stayed in one piece.

As I turned back I caught the sight of Spezia shaking his head. His brown eyes were flicking furiously from the road ahead to the rear-view mirror and back again.

'What's troubling you?' I said. 'Apart from the fact that any moment now you might get a bullet-crease along the top of your head?'

'I can't make it out,' he mumbled. 'Looks as though it might be a Volvo.' He shot a look in my direction, a fleeting flash of a look that said many things. But his voice maintained its expressionless tone. 'They can move nicely, some of those things.'

The presence of a Volvo – that made a lot of sense as far as I was concerned, but there were reasons why I didn't want to discuss the fact with Spezia at that particular moment.

I put a hand on his shoulder. 'Damn nice cars but then they haven't got you, chum,' I said. 'And for all we know it might be just the one man. Driving well is one thing, even in a good car. Driving and simultaneously attempting to be a nuisance, that's another.'

He nodded. 'I hope you're right.'

'Snap,' I said. 'And there's only one way to find out.'

'What you got in mind?' he asked.

'Just below Fiesole the road takes a nice hairpin to the left.'

He nodded. 'And there's the lane to Maiano,' he said.

I ignored the comment. Good observation, bad moment to discuss it.

'By the time we get there I want you to be a long way ahead of that car behind. Don't mess around,' I continued. 'Step on it. This time I don't mind how many regulations you break, all right?'

He nodded again, then swore. A few drops of rain had spattered on to the windscreen. 'Just our luck,' he said. 'Just when we want absolutely perfect vision.'

'Don't worry about it, Spezia,' I said. 'It'll be just as hard for the people behind.'

I turned round to look at the occupants of the back seat. Corrente was dabbing at his eyes with his handkerchief, Tozzi himself looked on the verge of tears.

'I'm getting out in a minute,' I said to them both. I patted Corrente on the knee. I was keen to make him feel involved in what was happening. 'I'm sorry, Gianni,' I continued, 'truly I am. Life can be a dirty game, and now it's decided to be dirty to you. Do me a favour will you? For God's sake stay low and don't move. Spezia can look after himself very effectively. You'll be all right.'

I turned round, flicked the Beretta out of its holster, looked it over, broke out the magazine, then rammed it in again. I held it loosely in my left hand and on my lap.

'You getting away from him?' I asked Spezia. My throat felt tight and dry.

He nodded. 'Seem to be.'

'Right,' I said. 'Here it is. Listen hard. You slow down

to near-zero just before the hairpin, and that'll be when ▮
disappear. Don't wait for anything. Just take off again a▮
fast as possible. You're turning to the left, so the doo▮
should close of its own accord. Hug close to the wall all the
way, move quickly, don't monkey around. When you ge▮
into the piazza at the top of the hill you go the end, cu▮
across the far side behind the parked cars.'

'If there are any,' he muttered.

'There's a discotheque and drinking-place for the fancy-
boys up there, Spezia,' I said. 'Maybe it'll be crowded,
maybe not. The chances are in favour. That should give
you enough cover.'

'What then?'

'You come down the near-side of the square, away from
the main road. With a bit of luck you'll be leaving the
square just as our friends are entering it. They'll then
realise that you've turned round. They should follow you
out.'

'And you?' he asked.

'Coming to that,' I said. 'You'll be coming down the hill
not too fast, and you have to do two things. First, you make
sure that they don't get too close. And second, you make
sure that absolutely nothing else is between you. Nothing,
understand?'

He nodded.

'It's serious, Spezia,' I said. 'If there's some maniac in
the vicinity in some flashy sports car, let him overtake, and
quickly. When you two come back down the hill I want
you nicely in line ahead. Got that?'

'I'm not a moron,' he grumbled.

I ignored his remark. 'As soon as you're sure everything
is going to plan, you go from dipped to full headlights. Just
the once, so that it appears you're preparing to take the
corner. Anything else and they may well deduce or suspect
that it's a signal of some sort.' I paused. 'Now here's the
funny part. You're coming down the hill, the road back to

Florence hairpins to the right so what you do is take the road facing you, the minor road signposted to Maiano.'

Spezia's face was impassive again. 'And you?' he said. 'You'll be doing what while all this dodgem-racing is taking place?'

'Me,' I said, 'I'm going to be doing a little shooting at the car behind.'

'Ah,' he said.

'Just tell it to me, Spezia,' I said. 'The way I told it to you.'

He was word pluperfect, recited it all tonelessly.

'Remember to get your speed up nicely as you come down towards the bend,' I said. 'Then really stamp on it onto the Maiano road, as fast as you can take it away. That'll put nice distance between you and the Volvo, and with any luck it could mean that driver will be taking the car quickly through his gearbox by the time I get into the play.'

'Where do we wait for you?' he said.

'Where you become certain that I've done what I'm about to do. Could be anything from one to five hundred metres further down the lane.'

He nodded. 'Could work,' he mumbled.

'Thanks, Spezia,' I said drily. We were approaching the crucial stopping-point. 'Keep it slow and close to the side.'

I tucked the Beretta away, turned round and gave the boys in the back a quick nod. The rain was coming down faster and thicker now, but the time for worrying about considerations of comfort was long past.

'Going,' I said, tugged open the door-release catch and tumbled out.

I hit the bank of the road with my right shoulder, rolled over a couple of times, then did a quick gate-vault over the stone wall beyond.

I landed on hands and knees on the other side of the wall, pulled the gun out of my midriff and listened as the

Volvo changed down for the hairpin. Once it had purred away, I scrambled along the wall until I could find a place to get back on to the road again.

I ran along the road, turned off down the lane that promised to lead to Maiano. Off to one side was a driveway with gates that proclaimed the legend BABY'S CLUB whatever that might have meant, and further down the lane was a post signed to the VILLA LINDA.

I stayed close to the wall as I moved down the lane. Beyond the wall the clumps of olive grove and cypress trees reared up out of the fields and out of the murky atmosphere like platoons of wild animals.

Once I was sure that I had gone down the lane as far as possible without losing sight of the main road as it approached the hairpin bend – then, and only then, I clambered back over the wall and into the olive grove nearby.

Time seemed to struggle by slowly, and the rain refused to relent. I kept one eye on my watch, the other on the main road. A car churned its way uphill, shrieking as it went into the corner too fast. The rear lights wobbled briefly, then it straightened up, roared off towards Fiesole. Another jockey showing off.

And then it was back, the Volvo no more than seventy or eighty metres behind Spezia.

He was beautiful, I'll have to give him that; if I haven't given it to him already. As soon as the headlights came on to full ahead I ducked behind the wall to preserve what sense of night-sight I'd managed to acquire. And then I imagined the scene as the Croma surged forward, roaring down the lane towards me, the engine shrill with effort and intended power as Spezia took it through the gearbox.

As soon as the Fiat's lights had flashed past, I poked out my head and shoulders, my right forearm resting on the top of the wall, all set to pump some bullets into the farside front tyre of the Volvo when it was thirty metres or so away.

Just one thing wrong.

No Volvo. The damn thing had turned right and moved off on the road towards Florence.

21

I SPRINTED DOWN the lane as though pursued by the hounds of hell and there was the Croma, two hundred metres along, its brake-lights bright, the engine idling in neutral.

I slipped into the front passenger seat and waved the Beretta under Spezia's nose.

'For God's sake,' I snarled, 'what the hell were you doing in Fiesole? The bastard must have read my absence as clearly as if it had been semaphored across the piazza.'

'Look,' Spezia grumbled, 'I did what you told me. Nothing else.'

'Never mind,' I snapped, 'let's get out of here.'

I kept the Beretta in my hand as Spezia swirled the car down the lane, cut right at a crossroads and took us down the hill to a point just below Settignano.

We tanked our way past the vast sports complex at Coverciano, and then we were back in Florence itself, not far from the centre and moving along the road that led between the football stadium to the north and the railway tracks of the Stazione Campo del Marte to the south, the tracks hidden from view by a high wall that ran its whole length along the side of the road.

Just as I was in the process of tucking away the gun Spezia muttered, 'He's back, the bastard.'

'*Non e possibile*,' I said. That brought the gun back into circulation as I jerked my head towards him. There he was, those eyes of his flicking from road to rear-view mirror and back again. 'You sure?' I asked.

He nodded. 'Hell, it's a Volvo.'

I turned round, and there they were, the lights of a car. I was well prepared to take Spezia's word for it that they belonged to a Volvo. He knew his cars, a damn sight better than any amateur roadster enthusiast might. Over a hundred metres behind, and the only point of contact on that road.

I turned back to him. 'Right,' I said. 'When you get to the end of this stretch, you're at the courtyard leading to the railway tracks. Stop there and slew the car round so that it's blocking the entrance. Just dive for cover. I'll take these two with me into the goods yard. You'll just have to do what you have to do to stay in one piece.'

He nodded. That grim expression of his was back, firmly stamped on his features.

We sped along the wall, braked sharply at the end, cornered at broadside, and the car came to a stop. 'Out,' I yelled at the two in the back seat. 'Run and stay low.' I was leaning across the back of Spezia's seat, pawing the door-catch with one hand and bulldozing them out with the other.

They tumbled out. I leaped out of the car in pursuit and left Spezia to do some snappy manoeuvring so that the entrance way to the yard would be blocked to the Volvo. And then I heard him scurrying away for cover in the direction opposite to that which we had taken.

Tozzi and the boy were trotting along in front of me like a pair of polo ponies out for an early morning canter. 'Get your bloody heads down,' I hissed. I grabbed each of them by the elbow and shepherded them across the railway tracks until we reached some rolling-stock that smelt of stale, damp biscuit.

We shuffled along the length of two coaches. The third we reached smelt of silage, but the hell with that. Its sliding door was partially open.

'Stay here with Gianni,' I whispered to Tozzi. 'Me, I'm going along the track so that I can cross and get back on to the platform further down. I want to come up behind him if he's monkeying about down there. Just like in the Westerns.' I gave him a quick smile of reassurance.

'No!' He tugged at my arm viciously. 'Let me come with you.'

'Don't be a damn fool,' I snarled. 'Just you stay here, stay low and stay quiet.' I pushed his arm away brusquely.

I helped the boy up, then hoisted Tozzi into the carriage, and slid the door nearly shut. No fun for them, the next few minutes would be, but at least they were out of harm's way and off my mind.

I crept along the line at a crouch, keeping behind the rolling-stock right to the end of that particular clutch of trucks. I moved round to the end of the last truck, well out of alignment with the offices further down the platform, peered out in that direction, couldn't see any evidence of activity.

In the business of getting Tozzi and the boy away from the Croma and hidden in the third truck, I'd lost track of the Volvo's movements, but from lack of engine noise assumed that whoever had been in the car was now out and about. Hell, I didn't even know how many people had been in the Volvo, whether – as I suspected – the thing belonged to Belmonte, or whether it was another vehicle altogether. And that was when a bullet sang past my right ear and the sharp slap of the explosion echoed between the walls that bounded the tracks.

I went back fast and low, moved along the depth of the truck and along the length, until I found the sliding doors. The wretched things were locked. And firing off the locks meant wastage of ammunition. I had no alternative but to get back. The boy was the person I was supposed to be babysitting for, and I didn't want him anywhere near the sort of action that we might expect. Still. Too bad.

I went back to the edge of the truck and fired a shot just to keep everybody guessing as to my whereabouts, then scuttled back down the line, trying so hard to move along on the sleepers and not the flint chippings between them.

I stuck my head into the truck and announced my presence before the two of them moved into hysteria or panic, then hoisted myself up. They were both standing near the door and for all the stench inside the truck, I fancied I could smell their fear even more acridly. I waved the gun at them and told them not to worry, then grabbed the boy by the arm, and pulled him towards the entrance.

'Gianni, just help,' I said. 'I want to get up there.' I pointed in the direction of the roof with the gun. 'Let's see you lock your fingers together, and for God's sake keep them tight.'

He formed a stirrup for my feet, into it went my right foot, and then I was reaching for the top of the doorway, pulling myself up with the help of one and a half hands. No-one was going to get that gun away from me then.

The roof was slippery with rainwater, no place for anyone who cared even mildly for the condition and smartness of their accoutrement, but the hell with that. I wriggled along until I was able to peer over the edge and saw him straight away.

It was Fosso. He was crouched low, moving along the platform and hugging the wall of the office attached. The fool was still wearing his dark glasses. And if that earlier shot had come from the man in the moon, I didn't give a damn. Watkins had a gun in his right hand.

Just as I felt confident of making a clean shot, he slipped into a door in the wall and out of sight.

There was nothing to do but wait. And think. He smelt rotten, that lad. All that business at the Belmonte villa had been as phony as the hair on the Bearded Lady. Linda Belmonte's eyes had registered too much fear, too much self-pity for there to be any chance that Fosso had been there at her invitation. The gigolo act had worked nicely, but only up to a point. The smell of blackmail had hung in the air too heavily, and Fosso didn't seem capable of stopping short of anything, even blackmailing a woman into bed.

I was just beginning to wonder about Linda Belmonte's husband when the glass in the office window opposite sprinkled shrilly on to the concrete platform and two bullets whined nastily past the top of my head. I made a great business of jerking my head up, let out a werewolf yelp, topped it off with a throaty gurgle and slid off the roof on to the ground below. A rail caught me across the thigh as I fell, but I didn't have time to worry about the sharp stab of pain running down my left leg. I straightened myself out, the Beretta held out in both hands in front of me, pointing in the direction of the office.

There were noises above me as Tozzi and the boy seemed all set to jump down and inspect me for pulse and heart-beat. I looked up and the boy's face was staring down. I shook my head at it, and it disappeared.

Fosso's voice came from the office. 'That was Mann, Tozzi,' he shouted. 'You and the boy come out quietly.'

Nothing happened inside the carriage. Good pair, behaving themselves. All I could see from beneath the truck were two large wheels close to my head and a pistol framed in the office window. Nice to shoot the pistol out of his hand, but that would have been merely counter-productive. Let's face it, you get a bullet in the head and one thing you're not going to do is make much noise. Even Fosso would have worked that one out, but in his mind there would have been doubt. I was banking on the fact that he was bound to look at his shooting in the most optimistic light. He wanted me out of the way, *ergo* he'd be happy to believe at the earliest possible moment that I really was out of the way.

Time passed very slowly, and then the shadow of the gun in the window went away. I heard scuffling sounds from across the tracks and his voice came through again just as the door began to swing open.

'Tozzi,' he said. 'You and the boy do as I say, no? You come out and move here slowly.' The voice was more shrill than the last time we'd heard it.

157

And then he was there, standing by the doorframe, those damned dark glasses still tucked around his face and a Luger stuck in his hand, pointing towards the coach under which I was lying.

Maybe his eyesight was awful anyway, but I decided not to make any experiments. I made sure my elbows were set firm on the ground, took my left hand away from the butt of the Beretta and put two bullets into him, high on his body and on its left side.

The gun loosed off a sharp burst in our direction, but the bullets were well over the top of the roof of the truck, aiming for Saturn or Venus or anything else handy. His body smacked into the door, the door smacked against the wall, and both became still in close proximity to each other.

I picked myself off the ground, poked my head into the truck and ordered Tozzi and the boy down. While they were doing that I crossed the tracks towards the office, the Beretta still in my hand. I knew Fosso would be dead, but one, you can never be even a thousand per cent certain and two, guns get warm when they're fired. The way I keep mine, that would have meant one hell of a hot groin.

I stuck a foot on to the side of his neck and pushed. The dark glasses half slid off his face, and this time his eyes made a better match than the last time I'd seen them.

I turned away as the other two came up to join me, grabbed them by the elbows before they could evince too much curiosity and led them to the car. Tozzi's face was damp, the boy's was pale. Which made it good to see Spezia again. By the time we reached the Croma he was behind the wheel and all set to go. He was developing into a regular little stoneface by this time.

22

I ordered Spezia to take us first to Corrente's flat. I wanted to leave the boy there so that he could recover from the events of the evening in familiar surroundings. Whisking him away into a comparatively strange environment would have introduced unnecessary complications.

Only when we reached the river did anyone speak.

'Who was it?' Tozzi asked. 'That was Belmonte's car.' He was leaning forward out of his seat. I put a hand on his chest and pushed him back.

'Down, Dino,' I grated. 'For God's sake.' I paused. 'Just one man. When last seen alive he was called Fosso.'

'Fosso?' He tried to sound surprised but his face, already pallid, went into super-shock, and he squirmed back into his seat more effectively than if I'd pushed him there again.

'Don't kid me,' I said harshly. 'You know damn well to whom I'm referring. Your friend with the glass eye, the one who kept tailing you, the one you wouldn't mention to me. That's who.'

'You're sure he's dead,' Spezia said drily.

'Decidedly dead,' I answered.

I turned back towards Tozzi. 'You and me, Dino,' I said. 'Perhaps it's time we had a little talk, don't you think? Just to clear the air a fraction.'

He made a great affair out of trying to look puzzled; but his complexion was a nasty pallid colour and the fear behind his eyes would have been obvious even to someone who had only recently met him for the first time.

'About you,' I carried on, 'but also to discuss what we

159

should do with Gianni here. And then there is Belmonte and the question of why his car was being driven by the man back there.'

We were getting close to the centre of Florence. The rain had dried away, but the surfaces of the roads were ink-wet and the tall thin rows of houses were finding it difficult to rediscover their own characteristics in the thick-aired atmosphere.

We crossed the river, went west along the Lungarno Serristori that lies just underneath the Belvedere and the Piazzale Michelangelo, and turned into the Borgo San Jacopo, one of the most exclusive streets in Florence.

Corrente's apartment was set on the third floor of an elegant terraced building with elaborate designs over pediments to doorway and window.

Parked across the street was the regulation plainclothes policecar containing the regulation fresh-faced *agenti* I had expected to see.

I reached for the gun in my waistband, turned round and made a heavy business of peering through the back window at absolutely nothing.

'What the hell is that?' I said to no-one in particular and slid the gun across to Spezia as Tozzi and Corrente spun around to see what I was looking at. His fingers clamped round it just as the pair in the back were beginning to reface the front.

'What?'

I peered again. 'Sorry,' I said. 'A false alarm. For a moment then I thought someone was sliding along the wall on the far side, and being damned stealthy about it into the bargain.' I looked at Corrente. 'Come on, Gianni. Sorry to sound like a nursemaid, but it's time for bed.'

I pushed a hand onto his arm as he reached for his door-handle. 'Not you, Dino,' I said. 'You stay with us, remember.'

I climbed out of the car, opened Corrente's door for him,

shepherded him across the width of the lobby and into the lift.

Moving across the lobby we passed a middle-aged light-weight with bright eyes and a thin mouth. He folded up a newspaper as we came in through the door, tucked it away in the desk behind which he was sitting and watched us carefully until the lift door closed.

I led the way into the apartment partly from a sense of duty, partly from a sense of curiosity. But there was nothing freakish about the place. Some expensive stereo equipment; many records and cassettes; a large television set; several handfuls of books on football and thrillers, one or two books on Italy and political science; magazines jumbled in a heap in one corner.

The walls were spattered with old prints, the floor covered with a large rug in blazing oranges and purples.

Corrente turned to me. 'I don't need room, I don't spend money, so why should I care.' His skin was pale, making his small features seem more delicate than they really were, and there was a tightness around his eyes and mouth that had not been there the first time I met him.

I put a hand on his shoulder. 'Gianni, I'm sorry,' I said. 'But the girl dying like that, you can't blame just me, you know. Maybe if I hadn't appeared on the scene, you must be thinking, then it wouldn't have happened.' I shrugged. 'It's hard to say. Perhaps not then, perhaps not in that particular manner. But there's a lot of funny business going on, too many people are keeping quiet about matters which ought to be brought out in the open.'

He nodded. 'Maybe I wouldn't have minded if I'd known her better. But we'd only met recently and for me it was the first time that I'd come across a girl I really liked.' He paused, then waved a hand across the room. 'Of course, there have been others. Here. In hotels. At flats and houses round Florence. But she; she was the first one to make me use my mind, even in a primary sort of way. Take that act of hers. The first time I saw it, I was appalled, told her I

161

thought it was degrading, that she didn't have to do things like that in order to live. She merely told me, as gently as possible, to mind my own business, made me see what a hypocrite I was being. Me, I used to love being praised for my football. The girls who squealed with pleasure, the men who were intensely jealous, the fans who give you their adoration – I used to love listening to them praise me. But the way professional sport is at the moment – isn't that more or less something close to degradation? We allow ourselves to be treated as morons, waste our spare time on useless pursuits, live entirely in a small, narrow, essentially unimportant world. We've got to the state now where the monetary rewards are too ridiculous. All the character is going out of the window. They give you cheap praise if you win, kick you when you lose, without seeing that in any situation there will be gainers and losers. And who can blame them? The journalists are bitter because they are the sort of people who would give anything to play like us, to become young and strong once again. And the spectators are asked to pay ludicrous sums to see us.' He stopped, stared angrily at me. 'And it was Giuliana who made me see all this more clearly.'

I nodded. 'It's an unjust world, Gianni,' I said. 'You have to accept that.'

'Accept, nothing,' he said angrily. He pointed a slender finger at me. 'Look at you, Harry. You obviously like to think of yourself as some sort of samaritan, helping people out of their problems. But people like you become insensitive, however strongly you try to resist the impulses that push you in that direction. You live in a world that is characterised by mistrust and continually invites violence. So what do you do? You take your money and run.'

He shook his head. 'That's just talk, Harry, all that drivel about the nobility of laying down your life for a cause. If you're genuine and the cause is genuine, then it works. But not when the motivation is mercenary.' He pulled a hand over his face, then gave me a gentle grin.

162

'I'm sorry,' he said. 'I have no right to preach. And I wouldn't have spoken like that to you or anyone a few weeks ago.' He sighed.

'How did you meet her?' I asked.

'Giuliana?' He sounded surprised at the question.

I nodded.

'At a drinks party given by some of the directors of Fiorentina. Why do you ask?'

I shrugged. 'No particular reason. Just curiosity.'

'It was slightly bizarre,' he went on. 'There we were in the changing-rooms after a home match and suddenly a posse of strangers came in and began introducing themselves to the players. We'd never seen any of them before. It transpired that there had been some sort of palace revolution behind the scenes. These people had bought up a whole bundle of shares and staged a take-over. Thus the party a few days later, a heavy session of Let's Get to Know One Another.'

'Belmonte?' I asked.

'He was certainly one of them,' he said.

'And the girl just happened to be there?' I asked.

He nodded. 'Wives, girl-friends, lovers, hangers-on. The usual contingent. Giuliana had been vaguely invited by someone – I don't remember who. Certainly, she didn't appear to know anyone there.'

'How old was she?' I asked, as if I didn't know.

He smiled. 'The same age as me, she said.'

'You didn't ask her?'

'The other way round. She asked my age, I told her, and she said something to the effect that she was the same.' He held his left hand up, looked at the palm, turned it over, studied his fingernails. 'God, I'm going to miss her,' he said.

I put my arm across his shoulders. 'It won't be easy,' I said, 'but try to get some sleep.' I moved towards the door, turned back and saw the fear coming back into his eyes.

'Don't worry about that,' I said. 'There are two men outside.'

'And the porter downstairs,' he said. 'I haven't seen him before.'

'Another guard, Gianni. Just keep your door locked, and ring me at the hotel if you need anything.'

He came over, shook hands, saw me out, slammed the door.

I heard him sliding the locks fast as I waited for the lift.

23

I PAUSED IN the lobby on the way out and turned towards the agent behind the desk.

'Just the three of you?' I asked.

He ran his eyes slowly over me, then stared unblinkingly into mine. 'Another one on the roof,' he said. 'The people outside won't be staying for much longer. That'll leave just the two of us. It should be enough, no?'

I nodded. It tallied with what Regalia had told me.

Spezia was sitting statuesque behind the wheel, his eyes flicking about quickly like pellets of mercury, the gun in his hand and both across his right thigh. Tozzi was curled up on the back seat, chewing brutally at his lower lip.

I climbed in beside him, told Spezia to drive slowly to the hotel and took back the gun. Tozzi's eyes widened as he saw it.

'Relax, Dino,' I said. 'All that's over for the time being.'

'And Gianni,' he said. 'Will he be all right?'

'He'll be all right. Regalia has detailed a couple of men on to surveillance duties. And he's detailed them well enough. The man on the ground floor knew me, didn't have to bat an eyelid.'

I ran a hand over my face, pulling the skin about savagely.

'You're tired.'

I nodded. 'Damn right. All this chasing around is exhausting. And this isn't an easy case.'

'How is it harder than most?' he asked.

I shrugged. 'For people like me, nine cases out of ten are

taken up with acting as nursemaid to morons.' I sank low into the seat, pushed my knees up against the back of the seat in front. 'Here's a quick précis of my last case. I'm in Zurich, just finished a job at a financial conference, when the phone rings. It's someone in Rome. A very famous American folk singer is flying in to record some programmes for Italian television. They want me to smuggle him quickly through the airport red-tape, take him into the city and generally hold his hand until the thing is over.'

I looked at Tozzi. 'Fine, except for one thing. The boy's charming, plays good music, sings interesting songs, doesn't spend his whole time worrying about the under-employment of his genitalia. But he does smoke pot. A disaster. I've seen the cops in Rome at work. They round up the hippies, lock them up in the Regina Coeli or the Rebibbia for a couple of months, and then get round to wondering whether the poor bastards really were smoking pot or not. Very funny, if you happen to be a sadist. I'm not, and I take a certain pride in my work. This boy of mine turns up with a whole caseful of hashish. The minute I saw the stuff I got hold of it and dumped it as far away from him as possible. He didn't even know that Italian law makes no distinction as to the type of drug people monkey around with: he was all for having his fun and paying a gentle fine afterwards. So I slapped some sense into him, tried to make sure he kept out of mischief, and put him on the plane back to New York still in one piece.'

'And,' Tozzi said, 'collected a few hundred thousand lire.'

'There's that,' I said. The second time in the space of a few minutes that I'd felt what integrity I possessed placed under attack. 'You trying to tell me I'm not worth the money?' I snapped.

He put his hand on my knee. I pushed it away. 'Don't

talk nonsense, Harry,' he said smoothly. 'You seem over-sensitive on the point. I wouldn't presume to make a value judgment of that kind.'

'Damn right you wouldn't,' I grated. 'Not after the way you've held back on me with this case.'

He made a strange sound in his throat, part fear and part interrogative.

'For God's sake, Dino,' I said. 'There are some people you can fool precisely none of the time. Me, you fooled for a few moments. But not for long. The smell of this whole affair was wrong from the start, my friend. All I lacked was some evidence, some sense of characterisation. And now I feel close to the answer.'

'I don't understand,' he said, looking at me eagerly. 'I thought you refused as a matter of principle to involve yourself in affairs that didn't attract you.'

I stared glumly out of the front window. We were cruising as gently as the traffic allowed it along the Lungarno Guicciardini. 'It was you, you idiot,' I said.

'Me?' He stuck a thumb into his chest. 'How, me?'

'Because I actually liked you,' I said. 'I liked the way you handled Belmonte. I liked the look of worry in your eyes.' I turned to face him. 'Above all, Dino,' I said bitterly, 'I liked the fact of your seeming altruism, your care for and worry about the boy.'

I lit another cigarette. It tasted even more foul than its predecessor. I screwed it out in the ashtray. Then I took the packet from my pocket, ground it out of shape, wound down the window and threw it out into the street. The anti-litter brigade would have been jumping around like dervishes at that. The hell with them. There were other things to worry about.

'You'll be smoking again tomorrow,' Tozzi said cheerfully. 'I know your type.'

I shrugged. 'In that, maybe. Not in anything else. For how long were you Linda Belmonte's lover?'

It was over-theatrical, I'll admit, the timing designed for

effect. He was supposed to fall apart and sob out his confessional. It came, certainly, but not in the manner I'd been expecting.

'I'm sorry to disappoint you, Harry,' he said. He gave a thin smile. 'I'd decided long ago that the time for openness had arrived.' He paused. 'The trouble is that since we drove back into town you've been so full of something close to self-pity that you didn't have time to notice.'

I scowled at nothing in particular. My face felt damp, but the car was not unduly warm. It was the sort of sweat that may still have been apparent were I standing at the North Pole in nothing but my underpants.

'How did you get on to that one, Harry?' Tozzi asked.

'A hunch,' I said. 'The first time I called on her she simply didn't want to have anything to do with me. She started out by acting like someone playing the role of a gangster's moll in a bad feature film. I really wanted her husband. But she made a great business of attempting to hire me to spy on him and I saw that she was slowly breaking up. An absolute war of in-fighting was taking place inside her mind and conscience. And once I'd made a little speech about thoroughness, looking deep into motivation behind cases, then she really began running all ways at the same time. So there I was with the thought.'

'And next?' he asked.

'Next,' I said, 'there was you, and only a few moments after I'd seen her. I arrived early in your office, perhaps only ten minutes before you did. But in that ten minutes I found a note about you in a book, telling us in what position you'd played your football and the clubs for which you had appeared. When you arrived I asked you the question to which I already had the answer. And you left something out.'

He was looking tense now. 'Which was?' he said.

'You mentioned your upbringing, gave me a resumé of your career. But you made a point of not mentioning the fact that you played for Fiorentina between your spells with

Bologna and the Genoese club, Sampdoria. It didn't interest me particularly whether you were good enough for the first team or not. What did interest me was the fact that for some twelve months – maybe more, maybe less – you were living here in Florence. Say early summer 1965 to some time in 1966.'

'Make your point,' he murmured.

We were coming into the Piazza Ognisanti. I told Spezia to park as close to the hotel as possible, switch off the ignition, and be patient.

'It's what I was referring to earlier, Dino. Your affection for the boy, which came across so strongly from the newspaper stories I read. It struck me as being something more than merely a professional relationship. At first I thought you might be homosexually attracted to each other, that all the coverage might be a giant cover-up operation to keep the matter quiet. But even that didn't ring true. And in between I'd remembered the two of them together.' I shrugged. 'Today's kids, today's styles – they all look alike. But these two kids were really very similar. The same build, the same sleek features. And Belmonte put the cap on it all this afternoon.'

'What was that?'

'The hell of a thing,' I said. 'I ambled along to the villa. She was there with her supposed lover, Fosso, and Belmonte came in at exactly the wrong moment. Not exactly *in flagrante*, but certainly enough to effect a decent compromise. He hauled off and started yelling something about a bastard child. And I was home. Dino Tozzi, illustrious manager of the local football team, had suddenly metamorphosed into Dino Tozzi, lover of Linda Belmonte – or whatever her maiden name was – and very likely father of her two bastard children, Gianni Corrente and Guiliana Soffici, both born on the same day.'

He didn't appear to be crying, but his hands were wrapped round the sides of his head, the fingers bloodless with tension.

'Just one thing, Dino,' I said.

'What?' he murmured without looking out.

'You've got two bastard children. How do you set about getting rid of them?'

Then he looked up, his eyes damp and agonised. He shook his head slowly, chewed his top lip, looked firmly at me, his mind seemingly at rest.

'I came from Bologna that summer, didn't know anyone at the club, not quite good enough for the first team then. Linda Soffici was living in a room at the house in which I had an apartment. Young, very vivacious, a student in fine arts at the University. We fell in love with each other on the staircase, were soon going out steadily, then became physical lovers. Suddenly, there it was. She became pregnant. The idea of abortion never crossed our minds. Now, they say, it's easy as pulling a toilet handle. Then, no.'

'You stayed by her?' I asked to save him from too much introspection.

'Of course.' He looked horrified.

'And no-one knew?'

He shook his head. 'Her parents were up in Bergamo, didn't express much interest in what she was doing.'

'And when the children arrived?'

'What could we do?' he asked, his voice plaintive. 'I had little money, she had none. I'd played a handful of games for Fiorentina, but I knew there was a good chance that I'd have to move on to another club. She had her studies to finish.' He paused. 'She did a crazy thing. She wanted to keep the children. I said no, that she should try to get rid of them. In the end she said she'd keep one at all costs, a reminder of me.'

'And you got rid of the boy?'

He nodded, his face miserable. 'That was her decision. She thought the girl more like me, so the boy went.'

'To Sardinia.'

He nodded again. 'The midwife who came to the house to deliver the children, she said that she could help us if.

ever we felt unable or unwilling to cope. When the time came we went to her and via some grapevine or other she heard of this childless couple in Cagliari, and took the boy there. We paid for her to do it.'

'And you found out where he'd gone.'

'It was incredible. We kept thinking about him, and long after we'd separated I'd wonder what had become of him. Then one summer I went to Cagliari and tracked him down. It wasn't difficult. His foster-parents were still in the same house. But imagine my delight when I saw what had become of him. There he was, in his teens, playing football with a fantastically natural talent.'

'And when the time came, you signed him?' I said. 'All the family back in Florence. Very neat.'

'We paid over the odds,' he said. 'But in all senses it was worth it.'

'And Linda?' I said. 'You broke with her how?'

He gave a quick shrug. 'An inevitability. For nights we cried into each other's shoulders. But I was being transferred, she wanted to continue her studies.'

'And Belmonte?' I asked. 'How did he come on to the scene?'

'About eighteen months later. I had a letter from Linda saying she'd met someone who would give her a new start. He was wealthy, not unpersonable. She wanted to get away from the past, she wanted me to know that I was the only one she would ever love, but that love was not enough. She was putting the child into a home, it was only right.'

'Strangely cynical,' I said.

'I agree,' Tozzi said. 'I always suspected that it was a precondition of marriage. Getting rid of the child, I mean. But that was her choice.'

'And Belmonte, did he know about you?'

He shook his head. 'Not then,' he muttered softly.

'Which is where we came in,' I said.

Two men had come out of the main entrance of the Excelsior Hotel and were staring idly round the square.

'Regalia's reception committee,' I said. I wrapped my left hand round Tozzi's right elbow.

'Come on,' I said. 'Let's go and face the music. And don't expect any nice tunes.'

24

I WATCHED THE characters at the hotel entrance watching us clambering out of the car. As soon as they were sure of their potential quarry, they ducked into the hotel and out of sight.

'The moment of truth,' Spezia murmured. He was on Tozzi's left, tickling the car-keys round the little finger of his right hand.

'Damn right,' I said. 'So why don't you clear out at the first opportunity and get some sleep? You'll need it.'

He nodded and we were through the entrance-way and into the lobby of the hotel.

They swarmed over us like hounds over a fox, perhaps half-a-dozen of them, with Regalia staying well out of spitting range at the far end of the lobby.

I was still hanging on to Tozzi's elbow and could feel his body tense with fright.

'Relax, Dino,' I said grimly. 'We'll talk, but under our conditions. And those are not these. And leave as much of it as possible to me.' And then we were face to face with Regalia.

To say he looked upset would be a polite understatement. His eyes were tight and fierce, the skin of his cheeks sucked in. His hands were both out of sight behind his back. A touch of the Napoleonic. But even Napoleon might have come out feeling sorry after a chin-wag with a Regalia in this mood.

I decided to pre-empt the situation.

'I'll talk,' I said. 'We'll all talk. But not here, and not

surrounded by your toadies. They impress the hell of a lot of nothing out of me and I'm damned if I can see any good reason for their presence, even their existence.'

'You murdered that girl, Mann,' he said, trying hard to sound sweetly reasonable and making a bad thing of it. The sweat was very noticeable on his upper lip, silver in the light, a pleasant effect of *chiaroscuro* against his dark, hard face. 'That's why they're here,' he went on. 'Protection for me from you.'

'Not me,' I said angrily.

'You killed that girl as neatly as if you'd thrown that knife yourself.'

'Let's talk about this somewhere else,' I suggested. 'Standing here is silly.'

'You'll talk where and when I say,' he grated.

'Don't be a damn fool, Regalia,' I said. 'No-one denies that the ball's in your control, but you're playing this all wrong. Let's talk by ourselves.'

He stared nastily at me for a few moments, then at Tozzi. For the first time he must have seen the bewilderment and misery on his face.

He turned his eyes away from Tozzi's face, barked some orders to the effect that his minions were to disappear in the direction of the offices across the square, and then waited until they were out of sight.

I nodded at him. 'Thanks,' I said. 'Let's go up to my room.'

He nodded, we made our way up the stairs and when we reached the right landing I told Spezia to make his way to his room.

'There's no point in his staying,' I said to Regalia. 'He was sitting outside in the car all the time, didn't see a thing.'

'You didn't see anyone come out?' Regalia asked Spezia.

The driver shook his head. 'The car was parked beyond the entrance to the club.'

'Damn careless of you, wasn't it?' Regalia continued.

'Why the hell weren't you parked where you should have been, somewhere which would have given you a good sight of the place?'

I made the interruption to save time, but it was a good point, one that Regalia had been bound to underline. 'We've been through that already,' I said. 'Nobody's perfect, and you can only park cars where there's room to park cars.'

Regalia grunted. I pushed Spezia away with a hand on his shoulder, and the three of us made our way down the corridor.

I led the way to my room, removed the 'Do not Disturb' card, kept the others back until I'd run my usual check of placement clues, beckoned them in, and rang down for some coffee.

There would be time enough later to discuss my impression that someone had been in my room since I'd left it that morning.

We made small talk until the coffee arrived. The coffee was fine, as most Italian coffee is, but the small talk had been artificial and silly, an uneasily-created lull before the heavy guns were brought into use. It had also been no coincidence, perhaps, that Regalia and I had been its chief protagonists, playing word-games with each other, both of us too experienced and too wary to pass on any information that was of genuine interest and might be cited as evidence in subsequent conversation.

'You know what this man did yesterday morning?' Regalia said to Tozzi. He shook his head in simulated disbelief. 'Went to Mass in the church across the piazza. Before he came to see us in your office. *Incredibile, no?*'

Tozzi blinked.

'Sorry about this, Mann,' Regalia continued, still refusing to meet my eye. He fished around in his pocket and produced two small books. I recognised them immediately as being mine, leapt out of my chair.

'Sit down,' Regalia shouted. 'I haven't finished yet.' He turned back to Tozzi.

Tozzi said nothing. Regalia looked at me.

'Simple,' I said quietly. 'For over fifty years people have been trying to write the Great American Novel.' I shrugged. 'Scott Fitzgerald said it all in the Twenties. I don't know why these other people bother. None of them can find a means of effectively expressing that bitterness, that romanticism, that poetry.'

Regalia smiled, a thin smile that was utterly devoid of humour. 'Fascinating,' he said drily, the smile wiped quickly off his lips. 'And this?' He threw my New Testament on to the bed.

Tozzi picked it up, looked at the spine, opened it. Even without the help of translation it was obvious to him what the book purported to be. He looked up at me in surprise.

'Same answer,' I said quietly. 'For me it has the same qualities of bitterness, of romanticism, of poetry.'

Regalia shook his head, stared at me with some bewilderment. 'I just can't make you out, Mann,' he murmured. 'You can't be that naïve.'

'I didn't expect you to,' I replied. 'I don't ever expect it from anyone.' I paused. 'And maybe I am. There's one thing I'm very aware of. For me, and for my breed, now is always too late. The other man has always stolen a march on us, always has the aid of clear-cut motivation on his side, whatever its colour, however evil its essential intent. All we can do is wait and watch and hope and pray. To lead that sort of life you become aware of your own limitations, you place a premium on self-knowledge.'

'Very interesting,' Regalia said acidly. 'So how the hell does all that apply to this particular business? Or does it?'

'Surely it does,' I said. 'For a start, I'm not the one who's been doing all the lying for the past forty-eight hours. Tozzi has, and Belmonte, and his wife. And possibly you.'

'Go on,' Regalia growled. 'Make your sermon.'

'No sermon,' I said. 'Just a few points, such as the red

herring thrown up by Corrente.' I paused. 'It stank, from the start it stank. All these people get threatening letters. Some are nastier than others, but we're only talking there about a matter of degree. The peculiarity about those that Corrente was supposed to have received was the running tide of passion in Sardinia for some form of self-expression. The claim made was that Gianni would be a brilliant feather in their propaganda cap. If he refused to play, then so much the worse for him.'

Tozzi and Regalia were staring at me with uneasy attention.

'First, I don't believe for a moment that any Sardinian, extremist or otherwise, would harm one hair of that boy's head. The thing would simply be a massive exercise in propagandist masochism, a classic example of the counter-productive. And second, I don't think those notes had anything to do with him. I was only shown one, and it's true that his name was mentioned. But so was Tozzi's. And once I'd put the puzzle face upward on the table I could see instantly that some pieces fitted very conveniently together. It was not Corrente that was being threatened, but Tozzi. And in that letter at least, Tozzi was the man who had done the threatening.'

'Get on with it,' Regalia said tightly.

'Here's the part you don't know about, Regalia,' I said. I flicked the Beretta into the open air, pointed it at his stomach and watched as his eyes tightened into venomous slits.

'No-one likes to have a gun held on him,' I said. 'I know that. But this little piece of information isn't going to please you and I don't want to see you making a damn fool of yourself.'

So I told him about what had happened after we had left the club. I told him in a deadpan voice, and he stared at me with deadpan eyes. But I was sweating heavily and he was flexing his fingers inside the pockets of his jacket.

'So you can thank our friend here,' I said, jerking my hand in the direction of Tozzi without taking my eyes off Regalia's face. 'He was the one who noticed that he was being followed by Fosso, and he consequently suspected that the skeletons locked away in his cupboard were close to being given an unwanted airing. As far as he was concerned, blackmail was just round the corner. How the hell could he handle it without bringing them out himself? Easy. He made the protagonist his son.'

I flicked a glance at Tozzi. He was sitting on the edge of the bed staring in my direction with eyes that were sad and mad at one and the same time.

Regalia's eyes were still impassive when I turned back to them.

'He brought Gianni on to the front of the stage and used his presence there to yell for help. And he sure as hell needed it, didn't he?'

Regalia raised his eyebrows.

'The knife-thrower,' I said. 'Fosso. He threw that knife not at the girl, but at Tozzi. He was sitting on my right side and that was where I heard the knife whirring past, not on the left where Corrente was.' I turned to Tozzi. He was pale and perspiring freely. 'In saving you, Dino, I ensured that your daughter was killed.'

He nodded, had to clear his throat before he could speak. 'I realised that later,' he murmured.

I turned back to Regalia and waved the gun around. 'Can I put this back to bed?' I asked.

He just stared bitterly at me.

I shrugged my shoulders, tucked the Beretta out of sight. 'So now,' I finished, 'you get your chance to tell me what little game you were playing on the side. And more to the point why the hell you're sitting there and taking all this so calmly.'

'You're forgetting Mimmi,' he said woodenly.

I shook my head. 'Not me. I never forget anything.

178

Certainly not events such as that. Say what you have to say.'

'The finger-prints you didn't rub off yesterday. We had a hard time chasing them up.'

'Now I see why you didn't beat me up just now,' I said. He nodded.

'That makes a lot of sense,' I said.

Regalia shrugged. 'He'd been following Tozzi, you say. Then imagine his surprise yesterday when Tozzi's office is invaded one, by me; and by two, you, a stranger who despite his New Testament and Scott Fitzgerald looks businesslike walking down a street.'

'Thanks,' I said drily.

'I was concentrating too hard on Mimmi, and the car with the two kids,' he said.

'The same with me,' I said bitterly. 'It was my first look at what I was supposed to be looking at and looking after.'

'So neither of us noticed whether Fosso was tailing us,' Regalia said.

'And he killed Mimmi why?' I asked.

Regalia shrugged. 'Maybe the boy spotted him, smelt something he didn't like.'

'Damn fool to let himself be caught,' I said quietly.

Touchy, that Regalia. He stared at me nastily. 'It turns out Mimmi and Fosso knew each other. Which explains why Mimmi seemed to have been taken off guard.'

'Well, so what?' I said. 'Fosso was the source of threat, Fosso is dead, so the threat no longer exists. Right?' I finished firmly.

And the phone rang. Hell, it was past midnight and well past the time at which civilised people make phone calls.

I walked over to the table by the bed, lifted the receiver as tenderly as if it had been made of Florentine silk and pressed it to my ear.

'Please come.' The voice sounded exhausted, on the verge of collapse. 'My husband has something to say to you.' And the line became dead.

179

dead, wishing that he had never existed. Everything inside me had exploded.' He took a gulp of his drink. 'And Giacon said he thought he could help me.'

'Help you how?'

'He'd heard of a man who would take care of people for money.'

'Christ,' I said. It was my turn to sweat.

'At first I thought he was talking about Fosso,' Belmonte went on. 'Then I realised he was talking about Tozzi and I was appalled.'

'You're not saying he talked you into it all of his own accord,' I said bitterly.

Belmonte gave us all a terrified look. 'Yes and no,' he said incoherently. He took another gulp of gin. 'He worked hard on me but I suppose I was ready to be talked into it.'

'And he did what?'

'After we'd argued it around for over an hour he took me back to his office and made a phone-call to someone in Milan. He scribbled a number on a pad, hung up, and immediately placed a call to Rome. There were people who took care of people for a price, he informed me. Just a few, a small handful who were well used, and suited, to constant travel and immediate call to work. I couldn't cope with what was happening. So I flopped down on one of the chairs in the office. I was feeling nauseous and dizzy. He talked very excitedly to the person in Rome, the fingers of his spare hand flexing and unflexing like the paws of a cat. At one stage he said, "Then it will have to be the Englishman." He talked for perhaps fifteen minutes, and made more notes. When he put the phone down he turned to me and said, "It's done." "What?" I asked. "For twenty million lire, half now, and half later, someone is willing to keep Tozzi quiet."'

There was a groan from my right. It was Tozzi's turn to hold his head in his hands. This was getting to be a Heavy-Head contest of some kind or other.

'Crawford,' I said to Regalia.

'You think so?' he asked.

'Must be,' I said. 'No other that I know of.'

I turned back to Belmonte. 'What else?'

'I wrote out a cheque for a million lire, and left blank the name of the payee.'

'And walked out, just like that?' I said nastily.

'You don't understand,' Belmonte groaned. 'I didn't think this man would harm Tozzi. Not really.'

'What the hell did you expect?' I said savagely. 'You expected him to march up to Dino with a bag of sweets and kiss both his cheeks?'

'Is it really serious?' Belmonte whispered.

'Damn right it is,' I said. 'At this moment an English gunman called Crawford, who can shoot the whiskers off a rat at three hundred yards, this character is wandering round planning the right moment to tuck Tozzi into limbo with a well-placed bullet.' I stood up. 'We're leaving.'

I marched to the door and led the way out into the driveway. There I waited for Tozzi and Regalia to catch up.

Regalia shook his head. 'Some people.'

I nodded. 'Thank God it wasn't Benkaddour,' I said. 'At least Crawford's a cautious bastard. That Arab would have spattered Dino into fragments by now.'

For a moment Tozzi looked ready to throw up, then he stood up very straight, held himself together and gave me a faint, weak smile.

As we helped him down the driveway I had the feeling that he was a man I was prepared to die for. Just for that one smile – a smile of romanticism, bitterness and poetry.

26

Tozzi slept in my bed. I peeled the counterpane off the top, snatched a pillow and made a make-shift bed on the floor.

It wasn't the most restful night I've ever spent. Twice Tozzi's nightmares woke me, twice I fed him some water, twice I told him to shut up and relax.

By the time Spezia rapped on the door at breakfast time, my face felt like a greasy cloth and there was an intermittent buzzing in my ears. Too much had taken place and too rapidly. I showered away the dried sweat on my body, shaved the grease off my face and changed into new clothes.

The three of us took breakfast in my room – coffee and brioches. Two cups of the former opened my eyes and helped to dissipate the muzziness inside my head. We ate and drank in silence until the phone rang.

It was a long-distance call from Paris and it surprised the hell out of me.

Claude Lasalle, one of my phantom companions. Only twice in five years had our paths crossed, the last occasion in Marseilles two years previously.

He was small, neat, efficient, irritable and irritating. But I had never come across anyone who could pull out a gun faster or use it more accurately. His main problem had always been what might euphemistically be called eagerness. He was a fine one for winging people first and gathering the information later. And the mistakes that occasionally resulted – those never gave him troubled dreams or sleepless nights.

'Claude?' I said. 'A surprise. Truly a surprise to hear from you.'

His voice sounded crisp despite the static on the line. 'Of course, something of a surprise, Harry. I wish we could see more of each other.'

'I know how it is,' I said drily. 'Why are you calling?' Me, of all people, I didn't add.

'Just a commission, Harry,' he said. 'Something's come up and I need help. Your kind of help.'

'Now?' I asked.

'Next week will do. You're busy now, no?'

'Could be,' I said cautiously. 'How did you locate me?'

'Just ringing round, Harry,' he said. 'If you are tied up now, you think you may be able to make some time for yourself soon?'

I glanced at Tozzi. 'Damn well hope so,' I said.

There was a pause. 'Perhaps I can help,' Claude said.

I thought round that one. 'Perhaps you can,' I said slowly. 'Are you asking out of a sense of altruism, my friend? Or is your project that important?'

'It's an offer, Harry,' he said coldly. 'You take it any way you want to.'

It would cost more money, but in the circumstances I didn't think that would prove too much of a problem. The important factor always had to be safety, and I knew I needed help.

I talked money with him vaguely, gave him no information, and then asked whether he would be prepared to come to Italy for a couple of days.

'Hell,' he said cheerfully. 'I like Italy and I like Italians!'

I gave him some directions, with which he acquiesced. 'See you tomorrow,' I said. We threw farewells at each other.

I put the phone down, promptly lifted it again, asked for a number in Amsterdam, and waited while the hotel operator tried to place the call. She didn't like that, the fact of my waiting, but the hell with her. Few of these people like to do the thing right through from start to finish. Always the quick coffee or cigarette or natter or something, just to make them feel independent.

A girl's voice answered.

'No Piet?' I asked in English.

'No Piet,' she answered softly. 'He's away.' She didn't sound as though she meant it.

'Just tell him it's Harry,' I said, and there followed a long silence at the other end.

Piet de Vriete, another of the number. Tall and wide with fair hair, blue eyes, skin that reddened nastily in the sun, and a personality in counterpoint to that of Lasalle. Piet often had a gun in his hand, but only when there was a good reason, and given the latter he was never afraid to use the former. He collected girls in the way some men collect ties, using several in quick rotation before discarding them all and seeking out a new collection. But they were never allowed to interfere with his work and I never heard of one that resented him or he them. I liked him a lot.

When his voice made an appearance it sounded surprised to hear from me. 'Harry,' he whispered. 'You all right?'

That struck me as being one damn-fool question. 'Any reason why I shouldn't be?' I said.

'Perhaps none,' he said. 'How can I help?' he continued quietly.

'Apart from the girl,' I said, 'how tied down are you at the moment?'

I could imagine the shrug of those strong shoulders. 'Just sitting in and around the Krasnapolsky,' he said. 'But big hotel work was never my idea of an exciting life. They pay well, but that's the only thing rewarding about it.'

'That dining-room with all those potted plants,' I said. 'Can you leave easily?'

'Of course,' he said simply. 'You're in trouble?'

'How much, I'm not sure yet,' I said. 'Lasalle rang and I've talked him into talking about it. But I may need someone else.'

'Claude?' he said quietly. 'When was that?'

'A few minutes ago,' I said. 'He wanted me to help him, and I realised that I wanted him to help me.'

'Fine,' Piet said. 'Just tell me where and when.'

I told him. 'Just one thing,' I said. 'You haven't asked about money.'

He snorted. 'It isn't important.' There was a click and the line went dead.

I put the phone down and looked at Tozzi. 'We're getting help,' I said. 'It may cost money, but every lira is worth it. Maybe Belmonte can be persuaded to disgorge some of his wealth as an act of retribution for the folly he's committed. If not . . .' I spread my hands and shrugged.

The colouring of his face was a nasty ochre. 'I'll pay,' he said quietly. 'I'll take your word that they're worth it.'

I nodded. 'And as for me,' I said, 'we'll talk about my money later.'

He began to protest but I cut him off short. 'You can't begin to understand, Dino,' I said. 'So much of my recent life has been spent in the vicinity of people whose personalities and morals I detest. You're important to me as a talisman that my life doesn't always have to be proscribed by selfishness and idiocy. We'll talk about the money later.' I changed the subject. 'When do we leave for Milan?'

He looked at his watch. 'From the *stadio* at eleven.'

I nodded. 'That gives us time to do what we have to do.' I turned to Spezia. 'Pack up,' I said. 'We're leaving. I'll see you downstairs.'

I waited for him to leave the room before doing what I had to do, shovelling clothes into my suitcase and checking my armaments over for evidence of misuse or neglect. Neither existed, but it is always foolish not to make sure.

Tozzi stared at me with dull eyes as I oiled my gun, tucked it in my trouser-band, and strapped the knife on to the inside of my left ankle. By this stage in the game he must have become punch-drunk.

Before leaving the room I made two phone-calls. The

first was to some friends of mine who had a flat in the Via Palestro, just round the corner. I was annoyed that I hadn't had the chance to see them. Apart from the fact that they were excellent company, they also brought and prepared some of the most delicious food I had ever tasted. I said hello, and, morosely, goodbye.

Regalia was altogether less pleasant to talk to.

'I hope to God you know what you're doing,' he growled once I'd explained to him the recent developments.

'I think so.'

'You're not sure?' he snapped.

'I'm never sure about anything,' I replied. 'Unlike some people I could mention.'

'What the hell is that supposed to mean?' he said coldly.

'Just this,' I said. 'You're good at your job, but this business may have stretched you wider than you'd really like to go.'

There was a longish pause, and when he spoke again it was with a tone altogether more conciliatory.

'I've got the message,' he said. 'You follow the thing right through to its finale while I stay here and do some babysitting near the Belmonte villa.'

'Something like that.'

'And you,' he said slowly. 'You know what you're doing?'

'Sure I do,' I said. 'But then maybe I've been in this game too long. Perhaps it's time to retire. *Ciao*.'

He began to speak again, but I put the phone down, picked up the suitcase, made sure I hadn't forgotten anything and led Tozzi out of the room.

As the door closed behind us, the phone began ringing. I ignored it and the query on Tozzi's face. I was sick of telephones and there were things to be done.

Spezia was waiting downstairs, the paper suitcase clutched proudly in his left hand. I paid his bill and mine, gave the cashier a big smile and shepherded Tozzi into the Fiat.

The character fighting the lion in the centre of the square

191

seemed to be still having a hard time of it. And on this occasion I knew that the grimace on the face of the beast was a snarl of anger, not a smile of apathy. Good for the lion, and, I hoped, good for me.

* * *

We went to Tozzi's flat. Spezia waited downstairs while I took Tozzi up and watched him putting things together. There were shelves of books on all walls of the sitting-room and very few that didn't give the appearance of having been read. Some nice prints, a catholic collection of records and cassettes, but nothing to dispel the impression of loneliness that Tozzi's face habitually suggested.

'Do we travel to Milan by car?' he asked once we were on our way to the stadium.

I shook my head. 'Spezia, yes. But he'll be the only one. I want you to travel by coach. It's important.'

His eyes betrayed anxiety. 'But you'll come with me?'

'Of course,' I reassured him. 'Just tell Spezia where he should meet us.'

Tozzi fired some details at Spezia, who nodded and looked blank-faced at the information.

'We're using the training camp that belongs to the other Milan team, Internazionale,' he said. 'Beautiful place not far from Como. Perhaps if we met there?'

I nodded. 'Fine.'

Many of the players had clambered aboard the bus by the time we reached it, some already playing cards, others reading, yet others staring nervously about them. I made sure Tozzi stayed away from the window-seats, but otherwise didn't interfere as he went about the business of finalising his arrangements. It was high time he reorientated himself.

27

WE STOPPED FOR lunch outside Bologna and just off the Autostrada del Sole: lean beef that would have pleased even Lasalle, and the wine rationed to one glass per player. Tozzi poured the wine himself, an act symbolic of the enforced paternalism of the way in which affairs were conducted within the club. There had been one ghastly moment just after Spezia had driven away in the Croma during which Gianni had alone failed to materialise. Just as I was beginning to fear that something had gone seriously wrong, his green Porsche screamed round a corner and shrieked to a halt on the edge of the pavement. He'd overslept. And he still looked sleepy during lunch, saying little and avoiding my eye as often as possible. He may have been feeling guilty about some of the things he had said the previous evening, but had no right to feel one fraction of the guilt that slung to both Tozzi and myself.

They both slept deeply as the pullman made its way north up the autostrada, waking only as we made our way through Milan and out to the north-east.

The training camp at Appiano Gentile was vast, an army of pitches, goal-posts, trees and chalets. Within a few minutes of arrival Tozzi was being quizzed by local journalists as to team formations and tactics, and his players were out in their track-suits and doing exercises.

Spezia joined me out of nowhere and together we sat on the grass and watched the proceedings.

'The boy looks good,' Spezia said after a few minutes of

the practice-match had passed. 'Sharp and mean. I haven't seen him like this for a long time.'

When the game finished Corrente pushed a hard look in my direction as if to make sure that I'd been aware of his mood. When I nodded, he gave a thin smile and trotted away to join the other players in the showers. Perhaps he was on the verge of making a formal offering of his talent to the girl he thought he might have loved.

The evening meal was tasty and quiet, and an early retirement to bed wonderfully welcome. Tozzi had the room next to mine, but he had become only one of my problems.

* * *

Spezia and I breakfasted with the players the following day and left the training camp just as they began a mid-morning training session. The air was crisp, the sun bright in a pale sky, the clumps of pine and silver-birch emerald against that pallidity.

We skirted the city to the east and arrived at Linate airport in good time. I left Spezia outside, told him to read a magazine and wandered off in search of a coffee.

Just above the entrance to the main waiting area was a weary notice — LA LEGGE ITALIANA PROIBISCE IL TRASPORTE E L'ESPORTAZIONE DI QUALSIASI TIPO DI ARMA SENZA AUTORIZZAZIONE. I wondered whether Lasalle and de Vriete would arrive complete with armament, or make a collection once they'd reached the city centre.

Two cups of coffee and half a crossword later I made my way to the viewing-platform outside. I waited until the Air France Airbus had landed before moving completely into the open. Lasalle's eagle eyes might have seen me from the runway. In the event I found a clutch of plane-spotters and, more important, their parents able to act as unwilling camouflage. I tucked a pair of dark glasses round the top half of my face, inserted myself into their midst and waited for the plane to taxi to a halt.

Lasalle exited from the Airbus looking foxy and stayed that way until he disappeared from sight up one of the ramps leading to the clearance area, his eyes darting around like bagatelle balls. He was carrying a slim attaché-case in black.

I slid across the platform, waited a few moments, then watched him move into a taxi and it towards the city centre.

A clutch of people walked away from the roof, another clutch made its way there. Twenty minutes later Piet de Vriete clambered out of the Alitalia DC that had brought him from Amsterdam. His hands were free. And as with Lasalle there appeared to be no evidence that he had been tailed, no evidence that he had arranged to meet someone at the airport.

Spezia, the Croma and I joined the cortège on its route into Milan.

* * *

Not surprisingly, the Ristorante Boccaccio is actually in the Via Boccaccio. The pizza ovens are in the centre of the restaurant with booths near the entrance-way for the short-order eaters and the area with waiter-service behind.

I walked past the fresh-faced girl at the till, past the booths, past the oven, tucked myself into the corner seat and ordered a drink.

I'd asked Lasalle and de Vriete to meet me there partly because the restaurant serves some of the best pasta to be found in Milan, partly because it was within easy access to the western side of the city, the one wherein I expected some action to take place shortly.

They both arrived early, de Vriete the first.

We shook hands, exchanged greetings and he stared at me rather intently.

'Bad trouble, Harry?' he asked.

I shrugged. 'Not sure yet,' I said. 'We'll see.'

'Nothing you want to talk about before Claude arrives?'

That worried me. 'You think there should be?' I asked.

'Me?' He stared at me unblinkingly with anxious blue eyes. 'I never know anything.' And Lasalle slid into the room, his paws sunk in the pockets of his coat.

More handshakes, more greetings.

We settled down, I ordered some food, some wine, some mineral water for Lasalle and he asked me a question.

'Money, Harry,' he asked. 'How much and when?'

I took some fifty-thousand lire notes out of my wallet, spread them on the table and watched him detach ten from the pile. 'As an advance,' he said.

I smiled at him. 'Cautious bastard, aren't you?'

'Maybe,' he said slowly.

I nodded at him, then turned to de Vriete.

'You, Piet,' I said.

He shook his head. 'Afterwards, Harry, when the job's done and well done.'

I waited until the food and drink had arrived, and then launched into the tale of why, how and when.

It was obvious during the telling that parts of the story didn't go down too well. Hell, I'd always known that the day of reckoning had had to come. But I decided to pre-empt the situation.

'That's it and it's messy,' I said. 'But one thing's clear. Crawford's already on his way to the starting post and no-one can or will call him back. Once these boys are contracted they become impossibly suspicious of any further communication. You know that as well as I do.'

'Just tell us the play, Harry,' Lasalle said quietly.

'It's this,' I said. I reached a piece of paper out of my pocket. 'Tomorrow Fiorentina are due to play a match here at the Stadio Meazza, and although these football grounds vary slightly in size and considerably in shape, some features are standard. One of them being the siting of the trainers' benches.'

'Each about equidistant between half-way line and goal-line?' Lasalle murmured.

'Right,' I said. 'They're nothing very special. Just room for about half a dozen people.'

'And that, of course, is where this Tozzi will be tomorrow afternoon?'

I nodded.

'*Zut*,' he said. 'So now tell us what's opposite.'

'That's the point,' I said. 'I've only seen photographs of the place. Basically it's a vast rectangular bowl with the corners rounded off and concrete terracing rising steeply above the level of the pitch. And right opposite the benches on which sit the trainers and reserves is a giant scoreboard.'

'Ah,' Lasalle said. De Vriete was fiddling with a toothpick. It looked like a splinter in his large paws.

I read from the piece of paper I'd produced. 'The width of the pitch according to my information is just under seventy metres. A hundred and ten metres long, sixty-eight wide. Between the touchline and the trainers' bench, another three metres, say.'

'And the width of the terracing?' Lasalle asked.

I shrugged. 'That I don't know. We have to account for that, for a few metres of enclosure, for a few metres of space between the iron railings that separate the spectators off, and the pitch itself. By my reckoning we're talking about a distance of anything between a hundred and ten to a hundred and fifty metres from the scoreboard to where Tozzi will be sitting.'

'A nice distance,' Lasalle said. 'What about cover?'

I shook my head. 'I don't know, but I'll guess,' I said. 'This game tomorrow should be a big affair. Two good teams, both near the top of the table. The crowd won't break the attendance record, but it may come close. Sixty, seventy, perhaps eighty thousand people could be watching and a large section of them will be making a lot of noise. From what I've gathered more than a few of them won't be averse to throwing a few fire-crackers and almost every damn one of them will be whistling, yelling or crying. It

197

means that you don't have to wait for home goals to get a lot of noise. It'll be there the whole time. And these people don't spend time looking at each other. They're concentrating on the pitch, where the real action is.'

'If Crawford gets tucked up by this scoreboard, he's at the back, right?' Lasalle said.

I nodded. 'He's in with the hell of a chance. The moment he thinks he's in any trouble, he can jettison the gun quickly.'

'It sounds possible,' de Vriete said quietly. 'But how can we be sure?'

'We can't, Piet,' I said. 'I told you that this was a crazy business.' I paused. 'But I don't see any harm in going out there this evening. It'll be dark, dark enough to feel safe but not so dark that we won't be able to judge for ourselves.'

'Any problem getting in?' Lasalle said.

I shrugged. 'A tallish fence, but nothing we can't handle.'

He didn't say anything. I looked at them in turn several times, back and forth from Lasalle's small features to de Vriete's larger ones.

I grinned. 'All right, so I'm mad getting involved. But this man Dino Tozzi is really someone very likeable, and how often does that happen to you, that you feel responsible for someone you can admire?'

They stared at me, stared at each other. Then Lasalle shrugged and de Vriete nodded his head slowly.

'Just one thing, Claude,' I said. 'When you arrived at the airport this morning, you had a black case with you.'

He stared back at me evilly. 'Bastard, Harry,' he said. He had difficulty in making his voice sound normal.

'Just wondered where you'd left it and why,' I said.

'A hand-gun, some overnight things,' he said quickly.

'And the former's in your coat pocket at this moment?' I asked.

'Could be, Harry,' he said tightly.

I nodded, then turned to de Vriete.

'And you, Piet,' I said, 'nothing at all.'

He gave a smile, opened the button of his jacket and spread the lapels wide. 'Nothing, Harry,' he said quietly. 'Just me. I wasn't expecting to stay.'

I shrugged. 'You want anything, you can have it.'

He shook his head. 'I'll help, and if anything nasty happens, I'll just have to watch, won't I?'

28

WE ARRIVED AT the stadium just as dusk was falling and couldn't see any sign of life either outside or within. Just to make sure that we were in with the chance of making a really smooth visit, I ordered Spezia to drive round the place a couple of times.

Cars were bustling along the main roads that framed the stadium and we met an ambulance shrieking its way with maniacal speed towards the hospital nearby. But close to the stadium – nothing. Just a handful of cars abandoned for the weekend and with no-one inside them.

We pulled up opposite one of the gates and waited. Half-an-hour went by. Still no sign of life inside the stadium. Finally, I turned towards the others. They nodded, and we were out and away, moving round the perimeter of the fencing until we were opposite what I thought would be the right point.

From the outside, the stadium looked like a geometrician's paradise with ramps running diagonally across the sides, six-high at any one point. It made for an impression of great height and solidity combined with a strange feeling of delicacy.

The fencing outside was perhaps three metres high, strong metal grilles sunk into a concrete parapet that circumnavigated the forecourt. Beyond the fencing was a ten-metre forecourt, beyond that the entrance to one of the ramps that swung sharply up towards the top of the stadium.

We moved to the fencing and examined it for footholds.

Nothing. So de Vriete and I made a stirrup with our hands, Lasalle put his right foot there and we catapulted him up so that he was able to swing over. The Dutchman in turn helped me up, then pulled himself up and over. He was a big man, Piet, and it made me realise how strong his arms must have been. But most of all I liked the way he landed in the forecourt, as lightly as a cat falling onto a carpet.

We made our way along until we felt close to the base of one of the ramps that would lead up to the terracing near the scoreboard, and then we began the climb, spaced out at intervals of twenty metres, myself leading Lasalle and de Vriete in that order.

We were well past the half-way mark and curving round sharply to the right when the flash from the piazza below caught my eye. I waved the others down, slid towards the edge and peered towards the source of the light. Then I realised that it had been Spezia, pushing the headlights on just the one quick once, flicking them off again suddenly.

We waited a few moments, and then realised why. A car was approaching along the road that led towards the city centre. It appeared to have the colourings and markings of a taxi. Its lights were out.

We watched silently as it drove round the stadium, then came to rest close to the place where we had come over the fence. Its engine cut out and silence fell again.

He waited five minutes or so before coming out. He closed the door of the taxi quietly with his right hand. His left hand was holding something, indiscernible in nature at a distance. The vehicle made no attempt to move once he had left it.

We watched as he made his way to the fence, pushed through the grille whatever he had been holding in his left hand and made his way over the fence. He didn't appear to find it easy. Once in the forecourt he moved round towards the base of the ramp we had climbed and disappeared out of sight behind the angle created by the corner.

'What the hell?' Lasalle whispered fiercely from close

range. His gun was in his hand, a Colt. 357 magnum with a four-inch barrel.

I flicked the Beretta into my hand. 'Might be Crawford,' I said. 'Come to do some reconnoitring of his own.'

'And I haven't got a gun,' de Vriete muttered mournfully.

'*Espéce de couillon*,' Lasalle hissed. '*Quel emmerdeur*.'

I assumed he was referring to Crawford below, not to either of us. He had a nasty gleam in his eye.

'Never mind him, Claude,' I said through clenched teeth. 'Let's move.' I crouched low and began to tiptoe my way up towards the lip of the terracing. The other two followed.

We reached the end of the ramp, bounded on the outside with iron railings, turned right away from it into the entrance-way, and there was a superb view of the stadium around us and the black shape of the electric scoreboard soaring up on our left.

I pointed towards it with the Beretta. 'I'm going up there,' I said. 'He should appear in the entrance at the far side and I'll aim to be above him to his right.'

Lasalle muttered something.

'You, Claude,' I said. 'Stay with Piet at this entrance. From here you have a good sight of the next ramp, looking across and down on to it. You'll be able to watch him come up and move into the stadium, but for God's sake, stay out of sight, the both of you. Me, he may be expecting. And I'm the one to handle him. You may be out of range.'

Lasalle opened his mouth as if to speak, then closed it again without having done so.

I left the two of them as they dropped into a crouch beside the concrete planes of the entrance-way and made a path swiftly up to the top of the terracing. The steps were steep which made it tiring and more easy to remain silent.

I slipped along underneath the lower edge of the scoreboard, and waited in a huddle just underneath its far corner. It was dark, but not so dark as to be blinding, and I was wearing dark clothing that promised to blend more successfully with the black of the scoreboard than with the concrete of the terracing.

Time passed with agonising slowness, each second being dragged to an unwelcome death. And then there was the scuffle of feet on concrete, and he was there.

His movements were slow, he was clinging close to the walling of the entrance so that the upper part of his body angled into view in slow-motion. And then he stopped and began to look around him.

Just one thing worried the hell out of me. I hadn't seen Crawford in the flesh for a couple of years, but I'd seen him in photographs many times since. The Crawford I knew had sandy-coloured hair, pale and thin. The head I was staring at was very hirsute and very black.

I put a bullet into the air a few centimetres above the given target and yelled, 'Hold it.'

He jerked into frozen immobility at the moment in which I began to rise out of my crouch, then his head ducked out of sight.

I leapt down the terracing, the Beretta waving in my right hand as I tried to maintain a sense of balance. And then there was a sharp snap of sound that reverberated between the walls of the entrance-way just as I reached it.

He was slammed up against the railings just outside, his hands coming round to his stomach, his head thrown back. From below came a crack like the sound of a hand coming down hard on to the edge of a wooden table. And then came Lasalle's second shot which took him high in the chest, flipped him over the railings and out of sight.

I stood where I was, lowered the hand carrying the pistol and the others appeared along the terracing from the far entrance, de Vriete in front, Lasalle behind. The revolver was still in his hand.

'Fancy shooting, Claude,' I said. 'I suppose you had to?'

He stared at me bleakly.

'That wasn't Crawford,' de Vriete said. 'He was carrying

a rifle-case, but that wasn't Crawford.' His voice sounded very unhappy.

'It wasn't, was it?' I said, my voice no happier than his. 'I saw him just before he went over, and the last time I saw him before that he was a Florentine sports journalist named Giacon.'

29

THEY STARED AT me in silence for a few moments, de Vriete unhappily, Lasalle nastily. Claude's blood-pressure was up, and that was not the only thing about him that worried me.

The Colt was still in his hand, pointing at nothing in particular, but with Claude that had never meant anything. Once he put a gun in his hand, he could cut loose without warning.

It was de Vriete who opened up the conversation. He was slightly ahead of the Frenchman and a step higher up.

'You been holding out on us, Harry?' he asked.

I shook my head slowly and slightly. 'Just a little, perhaps,' I said. 'But not with regard to this affair. I've been expecting Crawford all along.'

'Make any sense out of it now?' he continued. 'Perhaps this would be a good time to fill us in on everything. For instance, this Giacon character.'

'I told you before,' I said. 'What I didn't get across to you was my feeling of unease about him from the moment we first met.'

'Hell, Harry,' Piet said. 'That was a rifle-case he was carrying.'

'You sure?' I said.

'I am,' he said. He turned to Lasalle. 'You, Claude?'

The Frenchman gave a quick nod of his head as though he hadn't heard the question properly but was told by his subconscious to reply.

'Perhaps I ought to have made some connection earlier,' I said. 'Perhaps we all should have done that.'

'Meaning?' Piet asked.

'The last time I saw Crawford he was a lithe lad, moved quietly and well. The character we saw hauling himself over the fencing down there looked as though he was making very heavy weather of it, no?'

'So where the hell does this Giacon fit in?' Piet asked. He was fidgeting with his feet and his face still looked very unhappy.

I shook my head. 'He fooled me.'

'But the business about Crawford started with him, no?' Piet said. 'You only had his and this man Belmonte's word that Crawford was being called into this affair, right?'

'For God's sake, Piet, this is specialised work. You don't get lunatic pressmen going round waving rifles and playing at assassination.'

'Didn't that Regalia mention something to you about Giacon's army service?' Piet asked. 'How good he had been. A crack shot. Good enough to win silver cups and medals.'

'That was twenty years ago,' I protested.

He shrugged. 'You don't forget these things that easily,' he said. 'And you can bet your honour that he's been practising over the past few days.'

I tugged at my bottom lip with my front teeth. Claude was still holding his revolver and making a great job of saying precisely nothing.

'Let's take it slowly,' I said.

Piet nodded.

'Giacon was here on a reconnaissance mission, just as we were. So we assume he was planning something for tomorrow, right. He's a well-respected journalist in Italian football circles, and inside a football stadium he can get away with metaphorical murder. His rifle-case can look to anyone but us three just like some attaché-case. He has a press-card that can take him anywhere he wants inside the ground apart from the *tribuna d'onore*.'

'You're forgetting something,' Piet said.

'Forgetting what?' I asked.

'Giacon knew about all this ten days ago. Even more. Why didn't he make his play last Sunday instead of waiting for this match?'

'Just been thinking about that,' I said. 'So try this. At home, down in Florence, he's writing for the local paper. He's allocated a desk for the season, probably down in the front of the press-box, one of the plum seats. But up here in Milan, he's a comparative stranger. He won't be given a fixed place, instead he may well be told to fit in wherever he can. So nothing could be easier. He'll be in the bar before the game to let everyone know he's there, and the people he meets will naturally assume he's somewhere in their midst. So he can sneak down, wrap some dark or tinted glasses round his eyes, walk along until he finds the right ramp leading up here, get set by the scoreboard, wait for the crowd's attention to be distracted by a goal or some piece of hanky-panky and put a bullet into Tozzi.'

'And the rifle?' Piet asked.

I shrugged. 'Maybe he was planning to jettison it over the side of the terracing. People react with desperate sluggishness to any form of tragedy that isn't personal. You both know that. So he should have had plenty of time to make his way down the ramp and back to the press-box while the confusion was boiling up.'

'And you don't think this Belmonte was behind the play?' growled Piet.

I shook my head. 'No. I think he was conned by Giacon into handing over the money. That part of the story always was a touch improbable.'

'Damn right,' Piet said. 'Still, that takes care of everything, no?'

I nodded. 'Let's move. I could do with a drink.'

'We're not leaving yet,' Claude said grimly as I moved towards him. The barrel of his gun had flicked up and was pointing in the direction of my right shoulder.

30

'WHAT THE HELL?' I said. I took another step forward.

'Stay still, Harry,' Claude barked. 'Very still.'

'D'you know what you're doing, for Christ's sake?' I said. 'I'm not some two-franc bandit who doesn't know his gun from his nose. Put that damn thing down.'

He shook his head. 'No chance, Harry,' he said. 'Just shut up and don't move.'

Moonlight cut suddenly through a break in the clouds, emphasising the narrowness of his eyes and the lines at the side of his mouth.

'You're too good at your work and the struggle of living to be a joke, Harry,' he said. 'But many people find you droll, you know. You walk round with that little Beretta of yours playing at guns. But I never yet heard of anyone who needed to shoot hand-guns that preferred an automatic to a revolver. The damn things jam on you and your head's in orbit before you have time to swear about it. And there's your attitude, that's lovely. There's detachment and detachment, *mon ami*, but yours is something different.

'You're the kind of man who leaves corpses spattered around the place and they never had anything to do with you. You put a bullet into someone, then it was the gun that killed him. You push a car over a cliff, then it was the rocks that killed the people inside. You stick a knife into some ribs, then it was your knifeman's fault for sharpening the blades too good. Nothing is you, not ever. It's always *La Chance, La Fortuna* or Fate. Never you. You make the translation in your mind, shrug the shoulders and carry on.

But you can't afford to run away from your responsibilities like that, Harry, they're too important.' He paused and spoke to de Vriete, his eyes still on my face, his gun still trained on my right shoulder. 'What do you think, Piet? Am I not right?'

De Vriete made a great business of clearing his throat. 'You're right, Claude,' he mumbled.

'And you're the man to straighten me out, Claude?' I asked. 'To put me out of business.'

'Just out of business, Harry,' he said. 'But nothing more serious. There are people in London who want you back and in one piece. Some of them felt you were too good to lose when you walked out, and although they understood that you won't be up to doing too much fieldwork, you'll be valuable to them as an instructor.'

'You know what you are, Claude?' I said. 'Just a latter-day Judas, pocket size.' I could feel that sweat breaking out on my face, my neck, my back, between my legs. 'They finally got to you, didn't they? What line did they sell you, Claude? What rap were they holding over your head?'

'Shut up, Harry,' he snapped.

I shook my head. 'Oh, no. I'm working up a very nice desire to do some speech-making,' I said, and Piet threw his knife.

The bullet from Claude's gun burnt a scar close to my left tricep as his hand shot away from his body. Piet's knife sliced straight into the muscle of Claude's right forearm, knocking him off balance. He had been standing on the edge of the terraced steps and now he waved his arms around trying to maintain an equilibrium.

We watched him fall, then somersault. The gun slid away from his hand as he rolled over. And then his head went down to meet the edge of one of the concrete steps, he rolled down two more and was quiet.

* * *

He was still alive, but the gash across the side of his head was deep and while we looked at him his eyelids wavered slowly. The eyes didn't seem able to focus, the mouth opened as if to say something and then his head lolled to one side.

Piet drew the knife out of his arm and wiped the blade clean on his jacket. We stripped his pockets, found a wallet, some keys, a box of hard-nose bullets, a cheque-book and the open-ended return air ticket to Paris. I took out of his wallet the money I had given him and pressed it into Piet's hands. As far as I was concerned he'd earned it a million times over. I picked up Claude's gun, and gave that to Piet as well. He frowned, scratched his nose and eventually took it out of my hand.

I put my arm across his shoulders as we walked down the ramp and into the forecourt.

He gave me a thin smile. 'We'll talk about it in a minute, Harry,' he said.

I shrugged. And when we reached the fence he damn nearly threw me clear of the thing, he was so keen to get out.

* * *

'Just the two of you?' Spezia said as we climbed into the Croma.

'Just two,' I growled. 'There's no point in waiting for the third.'

He shrugged, fired the engine and we set off for Appiano Gentile. I could have telephoned Tozzi from the airport, but that would have missed the point, and I still had things to collect.

'In any case,' I said, thinking aloud, 'there's still the possibility that Crawford may turn up tomorrow afternoon.'

'No chance,' Piet's voice came from behind.

I shrugged. 'We'll see. We owe that to Tozzi.' I turned

213

to face him. 'You mind staying on for a few more hours and finding out? Finding a bed for you, that's no problem.'

'After tonight,' he muttered, 'maybe that's the least I can do.'

'Meaning?' I asked.

'Just think it out aloud, Harry,' he said gruffly. 'I don't have to draw pictures.'

'Well,' I began, 'there were those records, the ones from the switchboard in the Borgo Ognisanti. They really had me thinking for a time. Why two calls to London, the second so long? One call, that made sense. Regalia was merely trying to locate me, no. But that second call? And then I realised be'd been asked to call back once he'd located me. He'd discovered by then that I'd left Rome for Florence, and he'd been detailed to ring back. For some kind of instructions? It had to be, and that was the moment in which I began to feel slightly caught.' I paused. 'But I still don't understand the implications, Piet.'

He frowned, looked hard at me, then ran a large hand over the lower part of his face. 'That call of yours shook the hell out of me,' he said. 'You and Claude working together made no sort of sense. You never were his type, Harry.'

'Snap,' I said. 'Same thought, same sense of bewilderment.'

'And I knew,' he went on as though I hadn't spoken. 'You know how it is, how you hear vague things here and there. I knew someone wanted you, Harry, wanted you back where you were out of harm's way. But I didn't realise they'd go to these lengths.'

'I'm not sure they did,' I said. 'It's like some version of some traveller's tale that gets embellished in the telling. It becomes so confused that you even lose sight of the reasons for the embellishment.'

'And Claude?'

'He wasn't aiming to kill,' I said. 'It would have been the shoulder or the wrist on the right side.' I flicked the

Beretta out of its holster with my left hand. 'Silly of him to think that it would have stopped me, wasn't it?'

He nodded solemnly. 'Someone like Claude, he had to concentrate on the one hand, be so sharp with it that there could never be any competition.' He shrugged.

I smiled at him. 'Leaving us poor ambidextrous fools to do the best we can, no?'

He turned his eyes away from mine. 'You still haven't got the message, have you, Harry?' he asked. 'And it's not because you *can't* interpret it. No-one ever accused you of being unintelligent. Stubborn, maybe. Stupid, never.'

'Which is?' I said thinly.

He spoke very slowly, his eyes coming back to make a fix on mine. They looked harder than ever I'd seen them. 'Me, I think Claude may have had a point.'

'But you killed him, Piet,' I said. 'Not me.'

He shook his head. 'There you go again, Harry,' he said. His hand rocketed out and clamped my left wrist. 'I didn't mean to kill him, you have to see that. But he'd sold himself out of any sense of obligation by holding that gun on you. I wasn't going to stand for that.'

I wrenched my hand away, tucked the gun back in the holster. 'And me?' I asked grimly.

'It has to be up to you, no?' he said. 'How much freedom you can create for yourself, how fast can you run when the time really comes.' He paused. 'I think you could find yourself running fast and far, Harry.'

I didn't like the look in those honest eyes of his. So I turned away and stared at the road as though my life depended on it. My stomach felt very close to my throat and that had nothing to do with Spezia's driving.

31

PIET DROVE INTO Milan with Spezia the following morning, leaving me free to travel to the stadium on the Fiorentina coach.

I arrived at the coach early, grabbed Tozzi and the boy, and made sure I'd have their company for the journey. Things needed to be said, and I said them once we had settled in the back of the vehicle.

Tozzi was horrified. 'Giacon?' he said, his eyes wide with amazement. 'He couldn't have done that.'

'Maybe he wouldn't have done it,' I replied. 'But it would have taken God to stop him. So why the hell didn't you warn me about him earlier?'

'Come on, Harry,' Corrente said. 'He was a journalist, not some *mafioso*. How was Dino to know anything? Sure, he was a bastard, but this, this is something else again. Stop blaming us for your hang-ups.'

I scowled at him. 'You just say that again when we discover Crawford perched up by that scoreboard at Meazra.'

Tozzi grabbed my arm fiercely. 'Crawford? The English gunman? I thought – '

I cut him off. 'So do we,' I said. 'But I still can't wait for that final whistle.'

'You won't be with me on the bench, then?' he asked.

'Not me,' I said. 'I'll be up on the terraces. I'll stay until you leave the dressing-rooms, then tramp my way up. My Dutch friend, de Vriete,' I continued, 'he'll stay with you

217

right through the game, he'll stay the right side of you as you walk out on to the pitch. Just relax.'

We rode in silence for the remainder of the journey, and it wasn't till much later that Tozzi said what I'd been waiting to hear and what he wanted to say away from the boy.

Immediately after our arrival at the stadium he'd been swamped by journalists curious as to team tactics and busy inside the dressing-room giving the players a final briefing on the same. Piet and I had stayed close to him until he disappeared and then stared at our toes and each other in the tall corridor outside.

Now he came out, evaded a questioner, took my arm and led me a few yards away from Piet.

He stared intently into my eyes and murmured, 'Just tell me what I should do with Gianni.'

'Tell him the whole story,' I said. 'Tell him before he finds out from someone else. You're his father in every sense now. Maybe it's time to act like it.' My voice was nastier than I had intended it to be.

He nodded. 'You won't let me give you any money,' he said. 'So how can I thank you?'

'Don't try,' I said. 'Maybe if it hadn't been for me your girl wouldn't have got that knife in her belly. I don't know. But if only for that, I deserve nothing.'

'You can't blame yourself for that, Harry,' he said.

'I can't?' I said bitterly. 'You don't know me, my friend.' And then the players began to file out of the dressing-room.

I slapped his left cheek lightly with my right hand and said my farewells. '*Ciao*, Dino,' I said. '*Auguri, eh?*' Piet came over to join us and that was that.

I turned to look back at Tozzi as I reached the end of the corridor. He was staring after me with a damp expression on his features. And then I was away into the forecourt, past the posses of policemen and round the stadium to the ramp that would take me up to the scoreboard.

* * *

Scrambling round the stadium at night and when it was empty, and then this.

By the time I reached the entrance-way I needed, the players were on the pitch. Piet was sitting on the trainers' bench close to Tozzi and the noise of the crowd had converted the place into a madhouse. Whistles, klaxons, firecrackers and a lot of babble. Seventy thousand people make a fair amount of noise even when they don't mean to and this crowd did.

Just below me I spotted a clutch of Fiorentina supporters with their banners — '*Alé viola*', '*Gianni Corrente, siamo sempre con te*', '*Milan a zero, tutti a zero, Fiorentina a cento.*'

Overhead small planes flew past advertising whisky, hotels, even a private detective agency in the centre of town, their banners streaming lazily against the spring brightness of the sky.

I let my eyes wander over the people close to the scoreboard. No-one and nothing I could see that might be of interest. But I made my way there past fans reluctant to move now that the game had started and took up station close to where I had been the previous evening.

There's football and football. Me, I like the game a lot when it's played as it should be. It had always struck me as being the simplest of games, and the most admirable for that very reason. The accent should always be on speed, sleight of foot, quick thought. Of course technique plays a large part but, again, there are techniques and techniques, and that belonging to soccer is based not upon the whims of the people who make the rules but upon the players themselves.

What I was watching struck me as being the hell of a game. Those people who are supposed to know about these things had always been rude about Italian league football. The players played for such high stakes, they had warned, that the thing becomes too negative. All defensive formations and shouting at each other. No drive, no guts.

This was a game to prove them wrong. Milan had

immense players of immense skill, but there was no-one there to do what Gianni Corrente was doing for Fiorentina in pulling the threads together. Twice in the first fifteen minutes he passed the ball a clean fifty yards straight to his centre-forward in space. The first pass brought a corner, the second a beautifully-struck goal from twenty yards out.

Three minutes before the half-time whistle was due to sound Milan equalised. My memory of the incident is clouded by the fact that just as the crowd near me sprang to its feet in approbation a gun-muzzle was forced on to the back of my neck and a voice hissed, 'Don't move a centimetre.'

32

THE CROWD SETTLED on to its collective backside, the noise continued, the players moved towards the centre of the pitch and what had been laid on to my neck went away.

I waited a few moments, then turned my head slowly.

Regalia was lighting one of his cigarettes with one of those cylindrical French gas lighters. His eyes were smiling.

He blew smoke in my direction. 'Very good,' he said. 'I like a man who behaves when he's told to.'

I didn't say anything. The sweat was still breaking out of my forehead and out of my neck and at the insides of my arms. I turned back towards the pitch and watched the rest of the half in a crazed blur.

As the players trooped off the pitch and the crowd began to relax, Regalia's hand came down on to my right shoulder. I let it stay there, and then I turned back to face him.

'You heard,' I said deadly.

It took him a long time to answer. He was back in the land of gamesmanship. 'Maybe.'

'Christ,' I said. 'So when the hell did you start putting two and two together?' I glowered at him. 'And why the hell didn't you do it when you should have done it, which was long before it was done, like at the beginning of this whole business?'

He just shrugged.

'Damn it, Regalia,' I continued, 'let's just hear it the one time. You're glad to see me in one piece, you're glad to see me *here* in one piece, you're glad you haven't got me on your conscience. Don't think you fooled me, chum. That was you ringing back just as I checked out of the hotel, no? Just you making sure you'd heard right.'

'And you meant what you said?'

I shook my head. 'I don't know yet. Maybe yes, maybe no. I don't know. Peace and quiet are good stuff but habits die hard. You tell me.'

'The hell with you,' he said tonelessly. 'But if you think it was me that put Lasalle on to you, you have to be crazy, you know that.'

'Not London,' I said slowly. 'That's not their style.' I looked hard at him. 'Or is it?'

'Sudkovitch,' he said quietly.

I stiffened. 'That.'

He nodded. 'That,' he said. 'Ricketts never forgave you for that one. It was his big case and you fouled it up badly with your half-baked morality. You can't be surprised that Ricketts wanted you back where he could keep an eye on you and make you sweat it all out again.'

'Don't be silly,' I said. 'Ricketts is Ricketts, but he doesn't go to people like Lasalle.'

'Don't you be silly. He does if Lasalle walks on the same side of the street as you, he does if he assumes you won't be too wary of him, he does if he asks Lasalle just to deliver a message. His information on Lasalle was wrong. That bastard was no crypto-politician, just a trigger-happy torpedo. But maybe Ricketts couldn't have known that.'

'And he'll try again, only the message next time might be more subtle?' I said.

He shrugged. 'That's for you to find out, no? It's none of my business.'

'Come on,' I said. 'You're playing this too cagey. Let's have the punch line.'

His right hand dropped the cigarette it had been holding and disappeared into the pocket of his jacket. It came out with two small brown envelopes. Inside each was a bullet.

'Nice, aren't they?' he said. He passed them over.

They were different. One had come from my gun, the other from a larger-calibred pistol, a Beretta *calibre nove*.

'Go on,' I said tightly.

'Goats,' he said. He stared off into space. 'Funny thing about them is the fact that their flesh is the closest animal approximate to human flesh.' His eyes came back to meet mine.

I felt the back of my neck getting warm and damp again. 'So you took what decision, you and Ricketts?' I asked.

He looked shocked. 'Ricketts? Who said anything about him? No, my friend, not him. Just me. I thought it might be fun to have two explanations for Fosso's killing. Either he was killed after a gunbattle with some *carabinieri* using their regulation *calibre nove*. Or . . .' He didn't have to say any more.

The match had started again. For a few minutes I didn't say anything, just watched the play with unseeing eyes.

'You're a nice man, my friend,' Regalia said quietly. He stood up, held out his hand.

I took it and shook it where I sat.

'*Auguri*,' he said. 'You may need them.'

I watched him step his way down through the crowds on the neighbouring terrace, watched his handsome head duck out through the entrance below. And I knew that once that plane had left later in the evening for Amsterdam I wouldn't be seeing much of Italy again for a long time.

PHILIP EVANS

PLAYING THE WILD CARD

Gary Byrne was a footballing genius. When he was transferred to weave his skills for Fiorentina, the Italian fans
were soon calling him 'Byron' – a nick-name that suited
both his style as well as his romantic good looks.

But recently something had gone seriously wrong, and
'Byron' seemed to have lost form disastrously. Was it
simply the pressure at the top of the game he couldn't
handle? Or was there something else?

Understandably, Ross Armstrong, sent out to assess him
for a possible transfer back to England, is puzzled. But as
he investigates deeper into the case he finds himself inevi-
tably being drawn into an off-the-field drama of deception,
tragedy and violence.

'A crisp drama in the Dick Francis mould'

Financial Times

'London football club out to sign midfield star now in Italy
seeks low-down on his life-style. Insurance gumshoe opens
worm can of blackmail and bizarre sex'

The Guardian

'Inventive, well-researched'

Literary Review

'An intricately-plotted thriller'

Daily Telegraph

HODDER AND STOUGHTON PAPERBACKS